## DATE DUE

| | |
|---|---|
| MAY 0 8 2008 | |
| JUL 1 7 2008 | |
| APR 2 3 2009 | |
| DEC 2 3 2015 | |
| AUG 0 8 2016 | |
| | |
| | |
| | |
| | |
| | |
| | |
| | |
| | |
| | |
| | |
| | |
| | |

DEMCO, INC. 38-2931

# ...Now You See Him...

# Now You See Him

## Eli Gottlieb

wm

WILLIAM MORROW
*An Imprint of* HarperCollins*Publishers*

NOW YOU SEE HIM. Copyright © 2008 by Eli Gottlieb. All rights reserved. Printed in the United States of America. No part of this book may be used or reproduced in any manner whatsoever without written permission except in the case of brief quotations embodied in critical articles and reviews. For information address Harper-Collins Publishers, 10 East 53rd Street, New York, NY 10022.

HarperCollins books may be purchased for educational, business, or sales promotional use. For information please write: Special Markets Department, HarperCollins Publishers, 10 East 53rd Street, New York, NY 10022.

FIRST EDITION

*Designed by Kara Strubel*

Library of Congress Cataloging-in-Publication Data has been applied for.

ISBN 978-0-06-128464-9

08 09 10 11 12 ov/rrd 10 9 8 7 6 5 4 3 2 1

*For my mother and father*

In a fairy tale about beauty and love there is the phrase "he was not himself anymore." We long to be not ourselves. This is what matters most.

—*Andrei Sinyavsky*

# PART ONE

# chapter 1

AT THIS LATE DATE, WOULD IT BE FAIR TO say that people, after a fashion, have come to doubt the building blocks of life itself? That we suspect our food? That we fear our children? And that as a result we live individually today atop pyramids of defensive irony, squinched into the tiny pointed place on the top and looking balefully out at the landscape below? In such a time of dark views and darker diagnoses, I'll forestall all second-guessing and declare it up front: I loved him. I'd grown up across the street from him. In my own way, I worshipped him. With the slavish adoration of a child, I'd tried briefly to be him. Although we were both boys the same age and although we chaffed and teased each other constantly, below it all ran an awareness on my part that there was always something quicksilvery, musical, more sharply drawn about him that set him apart from the rest of us.

His name was Rob Castor. Quite possibly, you've heard

of him. He became a minor cult celebrity in his mid-twenties for writing a book of darkly pitch-perfect stories set in a stupid sleepy upstate New York town. Several years later, he murdered Kate Pierce, his writer girlfriend, and then committed suicide, causing the hot lights of the media to come on with an audible whoosh, and stay there, focused on his life, the town of his birth and, by default, we his friends and neighbors. In truth, it was fascinating, in a somewhat repulsive way, to watch how a lone wire-service story spilled outward, and the newsweeklies picked it up, and then, when it hit television, everything exploded in a bright and twinkling cloud of coverage. In the control rooms of America, apparently, they'd made the collective decision: *this is the one.* So within six days of the event, TV people were driving up from Manhattan and bivouacking in the Dorset Hotel, along with the big trucks with their sleek antennas and dishes, the over-made-up on-camera host women and anchormen looking all of them like something struck from the Stone Phillips mold and oozing a special kind of major-market insincerity.

For those of us who were his friends, even if we hadn't been in touch with him much these last years, there was the inevitable shock, followed by the inevitable (in my case) sorrow. For the rest of us in town, it was more about the transforming wave that ran through us on the heels of the media attention: that hot bolt of change that left us keenly aware of the way our bodies and faces might look in the rare air of television. By default, it seemed, we'd all become actors on a reality show dedicated to showing the rotten underbelly of innocent American small-town life. Except there was no rotten underbelly. This wasn't

Columbine High School. This wasn't that sandy sad place where poor David Koresh preached and died. This was Monarch, New York, a trim, proud little town on a hill far enough away from the major urban centers that people still pause a second to consider before they speak.

But no matter. The weather was turning crisp, the apples had already swelled, reddened, and fallen from the trees, and suddenly too many of us were outside braving the cold while wandering the streets of the town in pretend idleness, hoping to be on the nightly news. It was undignified to see Major Wilkinson, our World War II vet and a man rumored to have squirreled away millions in silver coins, buying a whole new wardrobe (at eighty-five years of age!) and posing in a photo op each morning at the entrance to the Krispy Kreme like a Wal-Mart greeter gone mad. Old diaries and dusty storage boxes were ransacked for sellable artifacts, and there was a kind of unspoken lottery that was won by Hilary Margold, who unearthed a tattered browning piece of paper with Rob's unmistakable high school penmanship forming the words "question authority." It was authenticated, publicized in the local press, and in tribute to the perennial American hunger for morbid memorabilia, ended up on eBay, where it went for a pretty sum. All of us, whether we'd known Rob personally or not, walked around with a strange lifted feeling, like a freshening wind was blowing, and maybe that wind would bring something live and new into our lives.

For my part I participated in almost none of it. I was stunned by his death, and then doubly shocked by the extent of the pain it brought with it—a sharp piercing ache in a private place, way up inside, that hadn't been touched in years.

# chapter 2

UNSURPRISINGLY, I SUPPOSE, MY WIFE, Lucy, has been less than interested in sharing my bereavement. In truth, she's never quite trusted the wildness of my old friend, or liked hearing the wiggy picaresque stories that, especially after a glass or two of wine, I love to recount about our childhood together: *Here's Rob and me at age ten writing and distributing a newspaper filled entirely with dirty words. Here's Rob showing me a new way to masturbate, which is "how they do it in China."* Not Norman Rockwell perhaps, but I confess I'm still a bit mystified by the vehemence of my wife's disgust. He was a deep friend, I've told her, part of the landscape of ancient memory, and I loved him the way you love an old land formation like a pier or jetty off which you remember jumping repeatedly into the cool, blue, forgiving water. "It's so simple, darling," I'd say, looking at the woman whose marriage to me has been a steady falling away from a dream of undivided light: "I felt really enriched by our friendship as a kid, and why shouldn't I honor those feelings as an adult?"

I've told Dwight and Will, our eight- and ten-year-old sons, stories about Rob, describing him as someone who was dedicated to telling us affectionately how lame we were, how silly, dumb, humanly wasteful to go through our days in a fog of nodding complacency and not scratch an inch below the brilliant surface of life. But being children, they're more interested—of course—in some of the spectacular scrapes we got into together over the years. And over the years, we got into a lot.

When I ask myself why the life and death of my old friend and his lover blew up into a rolling national media storm that is still, weeks after the event, engulfing us with battering headlines and high editorial winds, the only conclusion I can come to is that it must have been the universal appeal of the whole thing that turned people's heads. It had good looks, talent, the New York skyline and a bad end. It had boy-girl emotions, and even, depending on your point of view, a villainous asshole, in the person of a man named David Framkin. Some of us have advanced the idea that it was his girlfriend Kate's mysterious aloofness, her untouchable composure, that seemed to entrance the many men who wooed her, and that from within the illimitable detachment of her own death she was able—briefly—to entrance an entire nation. But I think at bottom the truth is much more mundane, and can be boiled down to one word: video.

Right at the height of the first wave of national interest, a cache of tapes of Rob and Kate was discovered from an unfinished documentary about the mystique of the writer's life, filmed at the art colony where they met. Nearly instantly they entered the special sad pantheon where that poor little starlet JonBenét Ramsey lives, along with Dylan Klebold, and even Patty Hearst posing with her machine gun like a porn star of mayhem and murder. The video contained several wrenching scenes of them individually talking to the camera about what they wanted to do as writers and with their lives. But I think the shot that captured the heart of America was the sentimental one of the two of them sitting in a place called Race Point Beach, on Cape Cod, and singing songs together, with Rob doing some fast-fingered chords on a guitar. It was old Beatles stuff, some Hendrix, a little Nirvana, but a big flaming brazier of a sunset was falling into the water, the waves were crashing off to one side, and as their piping little voices rose, twined and fell together in complete ignorance of what would befall them, it was impossible, watching, not to be a little sick with foreknowledge about it all, and to feel that maybe the best, most passionate love always breeds its own extinction.

For about two weeks straight, the tabloid TV shows were jammed solid with these *Unplugged* excerpts. Repeatedly we watched that fatally demure girl with her face canted a little bit off axis, as if looking, steadily, into a better world, and that guy with the striking good looks of a Kurt Cobain, but beefier, singing and pausing every few seconds to announce his thoughts on life with the impudent self-confidence of a born shit kicker.

Meanwhile, the literary community, roiled by the murder, mobilized to mourn Rob, while some of them, his supposed friends, did their best to distance themselves from the act. Benefits in his girlfriend's name were held to provide funding for victims of domestic violence. Others, predictably, mounted the soapbox of the tragedy to opine on the obscene competitive pressures brought to bear on young artists today. Semifamous people wrote strong columns for and against Rob in the *New York Times*, and former mentors of his lived the mayfly cycle of quotation for several consecutive news rotations. All the while, watching and listening, I took a bitter satisfaction in the thought that, if nothing else, and at least for a few weeks, the entire country seemed to concur with me that my dear old friend was unforgettable.

# chapter 3

NOT LONG AFTER THE MEDIA FRENZY ramped up, the phone rang at our house with Shirley Castor, Rob's widowed mother, on the other end. I hadn't talked to her in years, and I felt a sharp, not entirely pleasant pang at hearing her voice. She wanted to see me, she said, in a commanding tone that recalled the theatrical haughty lady who had intimidated me as a boy. Shirley was a controlling, unnaturally present mother who had fused with Rob in a way I'd vaguely envied as a child. He was clearly her favorite of the three of her kids. For several years, she'd basked happily in the reflected light of his success. But from the moment of the murder-suicide on, there was another woman linked far more memorably with him than his mom. In death, Kate Pierce had eclipsed Shirley forever, and I knew she didn't like that one bit.

I should explain that after Rob became well known for writing a book that, for at least one whole season, was the must-have fashion accessory on trains and planes for its "lyric anatomizing of the human heart," he began a new life which seemed to consist almost entirely of him moving in long, elliptical circuits through college campuses and art colonies, and arriving home about twice a year with an exotic new woman in tow. He came here to see his mother, and also to see us, his old roadies, at our monthly pizza-and-beer dinners, held by long-standing arrangement at a local dive called New Russian Hall. Most of us found it amazing that in the face of the stern challenge of earning a living, our grade-school pal had become not only famous, but on top of that had somehow achieved the slippery distinction of writing for a job. But we collectively envied him—to a fault—the by-products of that distinction: his conquests. We were awestruck by the beautiful young Turkish painter who moved through life doing the Dance of the Seven Veils with her hair. We were intrigued by the career novelist with perfect nails and a blinkless stare. We were bowled over by the smoldering, anorexic poet, and dear Lord but we were *killed* by the sensitive Winnebago Indian girl with the downcast eyes and the shimmering cataract of black hair. Each of these women, tense, gorgeous, and dramatic looking in entirely different ways, arrived in town on Rob's arm, took a look around, and did their best to conceal their disappointment.

Kate was unlike them from the start. She wasn't obviously an artist, to begin with. She didn't toss her hair, speak in a fake baby voice, or act like European royalty inexplicably fallen to earth among American hayseeds. A poised woman of about thirty, she was pretty enough in a regular way, affable but slightly cool, with straight blond hair combed so as to fall in two evenly parted curtains, modest clothes and a pleasingly upturned nose. Standing in front of you as self-contained as a vase, she smiled at you in a way that made you feel punched clean through with inner recognition. There was knowledge in that smile, otherwise kept carefully under wraps. And though we knew she was a writer herself, we were still deeply surprised that Rob had chosen her. Rob had always been such a strutting out-loud type in his own way that we were sure he'd end up with someone stridently beautiful or an aggressive social climber. Yet this girl, at least at first blush, was perfectly normal, the kind of forgettably average-looking woman you'd find loitering in an apron at the cosmetics counter, offering up spritzes of the featured scent of the day.

We were shocked when they swore eternal love, moved into Manhattan and began a life together. From that moment on, most of our information about them came from a guy named Mac Sterling. I'd known Mac—that grasping phony—since grade school, when we'd shared equal billing as "best friends of Rob." A big, loud, smart kid, he would later go on to be a top-tier journalist writing celebrity profiles in national magazines. I was always a little bit helpless in front of his obvious affinity with Rob—an affinity of wildness, as children, and of writers as adults—and after high school, Mac stayed more in touch with Rob than anyone else did. When Rob and Kate left the art colony where they'd met and planned to move in together, it was Mac, already living in New York, who visited them regularly and faithfully reported back to us during his return trips to Monarch to see his ailing mom.

Aloft on an updraft of love, the happy couple came

to earth on the outer reaches of downtown Manhattan, in some edgy neighborhood filled with the smell of fried grease, piss and poverty and that way the streets of New York (Mac talking now) reek from deep inside themselves in summer, their stinks activated by the heat. Rob had begun working on a novel for which, Mac explained, he was already under contract. Kate had meanwhile given up her previous long-standing secretarial job in Cincinnati and been able to transplant her skills to a rich lady on the Upper East Side who loved her dependability, her calm and her typing speed.

Outwardly at least, things ran smoothly for a while. She did her best to blend in among Rob's social set of grungy artist types. According to Mac, she'd increased the percentage of black in her wardrobe, and at Rob's urging had cut her hair in one of those dramatic downtown cantilevers that leans way out over a face. Her accent remained the same, as did the way she had of saying little and remaining poised inside the frame of her self-possession. But she'd begun to seem a little bit more subtly Manhattan, and less the Midwestern girl she was by birth.

The seasons passed, the leaves fell and in miraculous fits, in tantrums of green, they appeared again, and every day, Rob climbed to his desk like an exhausted swimmer battling the outgoing tide to the beach, and there tried to concentrate. Something, he reported to Mac, was off. The work didn't flow, the sentences built outward to no apparent purpose. For the first time in his life, his artistic nerve was failing, Mac explained, failing the way a healthy person fails into illness, taking their light and laughter with them, and the situation was all the worse because the expectations were running so high. Rob had never lacked for industry, and so he redoubled his time at the desk, roaring through draft after draft of the book and growing only more dissatisfied with the thickening end product. Maybe he was up against the limitations of his gift. Or maybe fame, in its suddenness, had blasted him right out of his formerly unshakable sense of self. Out, in any event, went the drafts, and back they came, covered all over with the penciled evidence of the editor's calm, sober and supportive no. And in this high wind of refusal, Mac said, Rob was beginning to panic. Because he wasn't prepared for rejection. It wasn't in the Rob Anthology. It was missing from the Rob Theory of Self. Misunderstood, yes, and important even. But rejected, no.

The only saving grace in it all, if there was one, was that almost no one in the wider world knew as of yet about his block. The city of New York tosses up so much noise and light that it's easy to pretend you're busy and convince everybody else of it as well, even if you're sitting all day in a box of squared failure and staring out a window waiting for the phone to ring.

Kate, meanwhile, had burrowed down into life and quickly found her footing. She loved the speed and efficient deployments of Manhattan. She found a cognate echo of her own ambition in the streaming, nervous vitality of the city. Every morning, she woke early and went to her millionairess's castle on Sutton Square, where she sat with perfect posture while typing 125 wpm and managing the woman's social schedule and fielding her calls. One day the woman, Annabel Radek, asked Kate if she'd like to stay on after work, because she was having a little cocktail party and there was someone there she wanted her to meet. After mulling it over, she said yes, thank you, and phoned Rob to explain that she'd be late that evening. And that was how she got to meet David Framkin.

The event was held in the double-height penthouse "library," with views, so the press later said, of both rivers. There was a guy playing the piano and waiters in white livery revolving around the room with tiny silver trays. The room was filled with that category of people who look like famous people, along with a few genuinely famous people themselves, and everybody was very stimulated and trying out their best looks, their wittiest lines. Kate had washed her face and put on a little bit of eye makeup, but that was all she'd done by way of getting ready. Probably she understood her role was to be social filler, and she did the best she could, circulating around the room with a little smile and making polite conversation, while occasionally refreshing people's drinks when the waiters were occupied.

About an hour after the party started, David Framkin filtered in. He was the famous corporate raider who had recently bought and bankrupted one of the city's oldest leather manufacturers. His preferred mode of operation, in fact, was to purchase heirloom companies, squeeze leveraged money out of them, cashier their employees, and then declare with a long face that these businesses were no longer "viable." He loved the word "viable." A balding fifty-something man with a big penguin belly, upswept gray hair, and an expression on his face of angry diagnosis, he strode into the penthouse, looked around himself, sniffing, like maybe the room was a day past its sell date, and then he went straight to the bar. On his way, he passed Kate, and stopped, drew himself up, and said hello. She would later confess to a friend that he was a "stiff, oddly formal man" who eyeballed her, she thought, with that important person's way of assessing the potential damage she might do him. She simply smiled and told him that she was Ms. Radek's personal assistant and had he tried the marinated porcini spears? A half an hour later, their paths again crossed. David Framkin had had two glasses of wine in the interim. He was a little bit warmer this time, and told her with a small air of self-congratulation that it was clear she was not a New Yorker, and he'd bet his bottom dollar on it. He leaned into her personal space while saying this. She was a Buckeye, she said, an Ohio girl. Holding her eye gravely, he opened his arms as if in ecstatic confirmation.

Two days later, Kate was sitting at the computer answering her e-mail. It was ten P.M. Rob and she had been fighting a lot lately, with him finding her "unreachable" and increasingly cold, and her refusing to "nurse" him through his extended bad moods. On that particular evening, an online glance at his dwindling bank account had triggered an irritability attack in which he'd flung a dish into the wall, and stomped off to bed early, leaving Kate to clean the higgledy-piggledy kitchen and eat dinner alone under the fluorescent bulb. She was writing to her mother back in Akron when a message with a corporate return address blipped in her in-box. Rob was sleeping across the room from her in the pull-out bed, and I like to think she turned and looked once at him, faintly lit by the lunar glow of the computer monitor, as she clicked and the icon popped open on her screen. I like to think she made some sign or gave some acknowledgment to his unconscious form that she was about to do something of momentous consequence. But probably she just clicked and read the letter from David Framkin, who wrote her, formal with embarrassment, to say he'd enjoyed meeting her and that——he hoped she'd forgive him——he'd had an assistant do a little research on her, and this assistant had found one of her two published short stories and he'd read it and loved it. He added in his rigid way that if she were interested in discussing it with him over a drink, he might be amenable himself.

AFTER THE MURDER-SUICIDE THERE WAS A WRONGFUL-death suit brought by Kate's parents against Rob's estate, and because the e-mail transcripts were eventually classified as evidence and read out loud at the trial, we know exactly what happened next. At nearly one A.M., in a friendly noncommittal manner, she wrote him back thanking him for his interest, and marveling at the fact that he'd found one of her published stories. After another sentence or two of casual chitchat, she said that yes, if he liked, she'd be willing to see him to discuss it further.

They met, Mac told us, two days later in a bar in midtown, a place that was plush with dark wood paneling and mirrors in the pretend Irish pub manner, even if the main clientele these days, Mac explained, was young hedge fund managers eager to drink fancy vodkas and wax expansive about the day's killings. As we heard it, David Framkin was nervous at the beginning. He was out of the carefully controlled environment in which he usually traveled, and on top of that was faced with the challenge of wooing the calm, perfectly contained person of Kate Pierce. Somehow or other, he managed, because they made a date to meet again two days later.

Of course, back up here in dozy Monarch, we didn't know any of this at the time. And ever since then, one of the things we've pondered is exactly how much Rob was aware of what his girlfriend was getting up to. Like I said, he and Mac went way back and they spoke to each other with the honesty of old lodge brothers. But Rob was a proud, stubborn man, and I think it would have been hard for him to admit, even if he knew it, that the woman who'd cashed him out of long-term bachelorhood could be wooed and won by a fat man with the grim, faintly pissy look on his face of someone who's just taken a bite of fish with bones in it.

But that was well in the future. At the moment, Framkin was still in the phase of meeting her at bars and restaurants around Manhattan, and doing his increasingly urgent best to reel her in. There is abundant testimony of waiters and bartenders on this point specifically, and they describe an older man bent always forward into the face of a girl invariably raked back, and smiling slightly. Meanwhile, predictably, the situation at home between Rob and Kate was lurching from bad to unbearable. His creative block was now nearly total, and he spent hours simply walking the streets, or getting so stoned and drunk at parties that he passed his days drifting in the long, slow curves of hangover. One evening, Mac showed up at our monthly pizza dinner and told us, shaking his head, that after more than two years together, he didn't think the two of them were going to make it after all. At the next dinner he quoted Rob describing himself and Kate as two people who over time had individually retreated toward the center of their loneliness, circling warily until that moment when they were finally back-to-back, facing outward, and every space on earth was foreign save the little warm spot where their tailbones met. After Mac stopped talking that time, there was a silence in which we all suddenly became aware of the rowdy sound of the jukebox and the low roar of chat along the bar. We tried to joke it off, but it was, we later agreed, probably the single saddest thing any of us had ever heard.

And then, like an explosion deep undersea, Kate's most recent story, "Bloodstone," surfaced in an important magazine that just happened—imagine that—to be published by a subsidiary holding company of Framkin's, and from that moment on, everything seemed to move at warp speed. In a matter of weeks after the publication, she was under contract for her first book of stories and a novel. Nearly as fast, Rob moved out—he found her publication a "betrayal," Mac said, of their unspoken contract never to let the accomplishment gap between them grow so wide that they couldn't shout across it and be heard. After roughing it on friends' couches for a few weeks, Rob took a tiny apartment near the UN. Not long after, he moved again, to a place on a far spur of Chinatown just under the Manhattan Bridge, where Brooklyn-bound subway trains rattled his building, and the Lucifer-light of passing cars shone in his smeared windows.

It's a sure bet that around this time he saw the (later)

famous photo that appeared in a New York tabloid and bore the headline "Say It Ain't So!" Grainy but distinct, the image showed Framkin and Kate leaving a restaurant. She was staring grimly straight ahead, and hurrying as she walked, and Framkin was hurrying as well, but with a satisfaction visible beneath his usual scowl. Indifferent to the accusations of adultery that would soon begin flying, his face bore the unmistakable signs of a man who, after a long slog through the dry deserts of marriage, has fallen into an oasis of sex.

Perhaps it was the photo that caused Rob's final unraveling. Whatever it was, we know he was spotted around this time at the Marx Bar, looking haggard and worn, and that he showed up once at the Pin Club unshaven, and according to someone who knew him, "really spooky looking." And then, for several weeks, he dropped completely out of sight, even to Mac, who tried repeatedly to raise him on the phone, and finally trekked all the way down to his smelly neighborhood and banged on the door, only to be ignored. No one to this day is certain what he did in that period, actually, but we can imagine him sitting for days in his miserable loud apartment as time slowed to a collection of long, slow thuds, like a heartbeat dwindling, and he stared out the window at the ceaseless cycling of city life. We can imagine that as the days went by, the discrepancy between inner and outer worlds continued to grow. The food turned bad in the sink and began to grow horns of mold; the bills were slipped hissing under the door, and Rob, the formerly important but now terminally stalled artist, simply watched, unmoving. Maybe as a writer he was used to seeing himself from a little bit outside his own skin, and found a certain odd familiarity in sitting silently from within a still point of expanding time. Maybe, for that, he wasn't even aware of having reached the apex point atop his mountain of woe, that tippy fulcral moment from which, with increasing speed, he began his tumble all the way down the other side.

# chapter 4

SHIRLEY CASTOR HAD ONCE WANTED TO be an actress, and as a kid, growing up, you could sense that desire lingering in the dramatic way she posed at the bottom of the stairs or walked around the house carrying her own ashtray, releasing extravagant plumes of smoke through her nose. My mother had once described her as a "Jewish woman," pronouncing the syllables with a certain relishing wonder—and for good reason: to be Jewish in the town of Monarch was as rare as being born an ocelot. On top of that, Shirley always gave the strong impression of knowing more about you than you did yourself.

I left work early, in time to make my scheduled appointment for the condolence call—a call no less necessary for being several weeks belated. Ever since she'd phoned me and that familiarly tired, dramatic voice had summoned me to their house, I'd been in a state of simmering low-grade anxiety. It was while pulling up in front of their home that the anxiety flared a moment wildly, and I found myself looking back across time to that afternoon more than two decades earlier, when I'd gone to their house looking for Rob. I had just turned twelve that morning, and Mrs. Castor, as if aligned with my festive mood, had met me at the door wearing something silk and faintly peekaboo, her eye watering in the fern of smoke from her cigarette and her voice mellow and welcoming as she'd informed me that Rob was at Little League practice but that I could wait. There was then a pause during which I'd become uncomfortably aware that she was looking at me intently, as if measuring me somehow.

"You can watch some TV until he gets back," she'd told me finally, detaching her gaze from me and turning smartly on her heel. I did just that, seating myself on the yellow shag rug two feet from their gigantic color television, and grappling with the brick-size remote in one hand. I clicked along happily until I found *The Price Is Right* and was just settling in when I heard her voice again, several rooms away, asking would I mind helping her retrieve something from the attic? I obediently got to my feet and proceeded up the three flights of stairs to the sound of her voice. The attic was an unfinished room with angled roof sections, and there was a line of shelves laid around the walls at waist height. She was struggling to move a heavy box off one of those shelves, and as I went forward to help her, I realized that below her sheer silk nightgown there was no bra, and that on top of that her breasts were not only visible, but as we wrestled the box down together, that they were somehow being *offered* me. We got the box down, and she straightened up slowly to thank me. Her voice had slowed as well, and she spoke throatily, complimenting me on my strength, and asking where I had gotten such muscles.

There was a strong sun shining in the attic, I remember, and the unfinished sharp tang of sawn pine boards and resin in the air. Mrs. Castor's lips were thickly red, incurved over her incisors, and as she bent forward through the air toward me I received the warm bread-flavored scent of her body. I knew her. I'd always known her. My own mother had once told me proudly that Mrs. Castor, who she feared and admired, treated me "like her own son." This was supposed to be a positive achievement; it was supposed to signal something surpassingly wholesome, neighborly and nice, and yet my erection at that moment in the attic was so fearless, so total in its claim on me, that if I opened my mouth to answer her question I was sure my penis would have leaped from between my lips like a giant megaphone and shouted out something insanely sexual at fatal volume. Instead I clamped down hard inside myself and turned away, muttering meekly about gym class. She saw, of course, and I heard her soft, girlish giggle as I went down the stairs.

More than twenty years later, I stood in front of their house trying to cleanse my mind of these deranging memories. I was still working on it when the door opened with a catty yowl.

"Ah, it's you," she said, peering out at me. The cigarette was still going, unextinguished, but as the door swung wider I observed that her entire face and body appeared to have taken one step back and fallen down on her bones.

She let me in, nodding sadly, a tall iced drink in her

hand. I tried not to notice the way the interior of the house had that creepy feeling you sometimes get when everything is like it once was, but shadowed and webby with age, and you realize you've stepped into the end of someone's story that was once the beginning of yours, and that fact can't help but make you thoughtful, and a little sad as well. But I was determined to be kind. This was the Castor family matriarch, after all, even if it was clear from the shakily applied hoop of lipstick on her mouth and the sloppy auroras of blue eye shadow, that she was drunk.

"So here we are, darling," she said. "Isn't it all dreadful? Sit down on the couch. Would you like something to drink?" She gestured shakily with the glass. "No? *Quel dommage.*"

She sat down on an overstuffed chair, facing me. There was a pause, during which I cleared my throat.

"I'm so very sorry," I began.

She nodded, staring at me.

"It's almost inconceivable," I went on softly, "what you must be going through."

She nodded again, somewhat wearily.

"None of us knew that he was in that much pain," I said, "or we might have done something, though I don't know what."

Pushing out her lips as if to admit that this, at least, was a slightly new wrinkle in condolences she'd heard a thousand times, she nodded again and then said calmly, "Me."

"You?"

"Yes. Why don't you ever come by to see me, Nick?"

I furrowed my brows, bewildered. But before I could say anything more, she put a long, knobbed finger to her lips. Veins swirled upward toward its tip like the lines on a barber pole. "Never mind," she whispered. After a few seconds of silence, she put the finger down.

"Do you think about him?" she asked, taking a deep slug from her drink.

"About Rob—omigod yes. All the time, actually."

She smiled, settling back in her chair.

"You were best friends," she said, as if to prompt me.

"For years," I said.

"What else?"

"I'm not sure how you mean," I said, wanting to oblige but a bit bewildered. "Okay." I rubbed my forehead. "I suppose he was a teacher, in a way. But he was also a kind of copilot for me in life, growing up especially. He was one of the smartest, most generous people I've ever met. Is this what you mean? Uh, Mrs. Castor?"

She was staring over my head, into the middle distance. "From the beginning," she said in the strong, tranced voice of someone launching themselves on a rehearsed speech, "that child could make me scream with laughter easier than anyone else in the world." She lowered her eyes and leaned forward confidingly. "These things are chemical, between mother and son, you know. They're already done—signed, sealed and delivered in the womb." She looked at me with a fresh alertness. "Do you believe that boys come into the world for their mothers, and girls for their fathers?"

"That's an interesting question, actually. I'm not sure I know."

She took yet another long, swilling drink and put the glass down on the chair with a loud crack, clearly energized.

"Isn't it true that one's spiritual father is more important than one's biological father, and the semen donor otherwise known as 'Daddy' is small beer compared to the truth of the person who raises you?"

"Where are you—"

"Going with this? Do you believe," her voice had risen nearly to a shout, "that one can have a genetic memory, and be tied to parents they never even knew?"

"I confess, Mrs. Castor," I said, choosing my words with care, "that I'm at a bit of a loss just now, and can't figure out what this is all about."

"You're right," she said, lapsing suddenly back into her chair. "Why am I burdening your happy little life with all this awful stuff? I'm sorry. I get these kinds of spells sometimes. How are you, my dear?"

Again, just as I had five minutes earlier, I said slowly, "I'm fine."

"Oh good. And your wife, what's her name?"

"Lucy? Fine, thanks."

"You have children, don't you."

"Yes."

Another pause. "Did you know," she asked, "that I was raised in San Francisco myself?"

"I think I did," I said, and lifted my eyes. Through the dusty venetian blinds, the sunshine and with it the day itself suddenly seemed very far away.

"With seals and sea fogs," she went on, staring at the spot in space above my head, "and oodles of interesting people? We had a home like a museum. Daddy was an insurance agent, but he lived for opera and Shakespeare. It was not in the cards, I'm saying, that I would end up freezing out here in a cold little hole a million miles from nowhere." She swung her glass around in an illustration of "nowhere" and in the process spilled some of her drink onto the floor.

"So can you blame me really if I didn't pass around the 'welcome wagon,' and volunteer at the PTA, and do the social thing with those dreadful matrons who always vote Republican and make my skin crawl? Of course, from my husband's point of view, Monarch was the center of the world. Yes, ring the bells, the lord and master has pronounced Monarch the culture capital of upper New York state! But then again, owning a hardware store does not acquaint you with the finer things of life, does it?"

She seemed to be waiting for my response.

"I don't know," I said, "does it?"

As I watched, slowly, steadily, deliberately, her lips drew back over long teeth in a crooked smile. I felt a strange shiver, there, in the shadowy room.

"Nicholas," she said, using the long form of my name, which no one ever did, "I would so love for us to have a candid conversation one day."

"Fine," I said. "What about?"

"Oh, things."

"I'm amenable," I said as cheerfully as I could, despite feeling myself filling inexplicably with a black, chill dread.

"Good," she said, and looked at me intently for a moment before her expression softened. "But that's for another time. For now, let's chat about the other man in my life, my poor dim Hiram. With Rob gone I've begun thinking of him lots."

Hiram was Rob's baby brother.

"I'm sure you have."

"Let's talk"—she gestured in a wide trembling arc—
"about agronomy as a major in college. Or about someone
raised in the lap of culture heading for *shrubbery*"—she
grimaced—"as a life choice. What do you think of that?"

"I think Hiram is a great guy. There's nothing wrong
with that, is there?"

"Only if you're his mother. But you!" she cried suddenly, now weaving slightly, even though sitting down, her
bust describing small quaking ellipses in the air. "You," she
said, though with less conviction, and then seemed to look
a moment at her drink, curiously. "Cheap," she said, "but
strong." With shaky dignity, she put the tumbler down.
She shut her eyes, and for a moment I thought she'd fallen
asleep. But then the eyes flew open.

"I always thought," she said, "that a person was given
only that which they could carry in life. It's not true!" she
shouted. "What I've been saddled with no woman should
have to bear!"

She grew silent again. Her energy was playing out in
flurries, like that of a fighting fish. I decided it was time
to go, before she passed out, or worse. But before I left I
needed to say something, get something off my chest. I
leaned forward.

"It's impossible for you to know what Rob meant to me
and to all of us who knew him, Mrs. Castor," I said in a
soft, urgent voice. "No one will ever understand what he
brought into our lives. But it was something about fear-
lessness, maybe, and going for it no matter the odds. It
was something about integrity and originality. I don't want
to sound like a Nike commercial, Mrs. Castor, but there

really was no one else like Rob. He's the most important
friend I've ever had, and ever will."

She shut her eyes and nodded.

"Lovely," she said.

I straightened up, feeling slightly relieved.

"But not enough," she went on.

Still smiling, I froze. "Excuse me?"

"'Like a whore, I unpack my heart with words,' said
Hamlet. Do you know what that means?"

"Are you insulting me, Mrs. Castor?"

"Don't be petty, Nick. Of course I am. I'm not interested
in your grief today, little man. In fact, I'm not interested in
anything to do with you. I thought a conversation with you
would be important somehow, but I was wrong. So, go.
Just go!" she cried suddenly. "Flutter off back to your life.
I should never have called, and I never will again."

I stood a moment, too stunned to be angry, and then
came to my senses and walked swiftly down the hallway
and out the front door. She'd called me, it occurred to
me, for the express purpose of wounding me as deeply
as possible. I thought I heard her singing something loud
and off-key as I hastened across the lawn. Once in my car,
I began driving home, swiftly, as if to outdistance something that was gaining on me.

## chapter 5

IN ENSUING WEEKS, EVEN AFTER THE TV trucks finally slithered away and the anchorpeople packed up and left, the town remained slightly altered, a touch bewildered. We all commented on that fact. It was the new watchfulness that had stolen over us. It was the way in which, in the aftermath of all that glary media attention, we felt ourselves looking on at everything as if perched slightly outside our own bodies. At the same time, there was the roused feeling of election to it, like we were special somehow. But as more than one of us said to another, Special, dear God, for what?

As the weeks went by, and things finally relaxed and the weather grew colder, we told ourselves that we were glad to have our town back, and our unclogged city streets, and the open spaces of our afternoons. But then the *New York Times Magazine* published a nasty, in-depth "investigative" article on Rob and Kate called "Literary Labor Lost: The

Rob Castor/Kate Pierce Story." It laid a heavy emphasis on the selfishness and egos of everyone concerned, and a great wave of tired outside attention crashed over us yet again, and for one week we wondered if we weren't right back where we'd started.

We were collectively like a hooker angry with the life she leads who is nonetheless rouged and waiting and open for business. We hungered for the media attention, I mean, even as we pretended otherwise. We saw the recognition as deserved, at bottom. It seemed validation for how each of us felt ourselves going along in our lives with some secret rind of personal value not yet noticed by the world, and still awaiting its moment in poignant close-up.

But we were also outraged by the *New York Times* article, plain and simple. We hastily reconvened an "emergency session" in New Russian Hall, where we spent a long and stormy evening debating what to do by way of response. We admitted the journalist got the look of Monarch right, with its graceful grid of streets, its historic redbrick district and its church on a gentle rise. She got the easeful style of daily life here right, and the way, for example, that at the high school gym, birdsong floats in the open windows over the thwack of the ball against the backboard. She even got how Monarch Mountain broods over the town all day long.

But no one had ever said before that "The shadow the mountain casts seems to extend even to the waking life of the citizens of this spotless, yet somehow morbid little exurb." No one had ever said, "The citizens of Monarch exemplify the staunch Babbitry of small-town American life."

And no one, most of all, had ever said, "At bottom, Rob Castor cannot be blamed for wanting to put as much distance as possible between himself and the place of his birth."

There was a silence after Mac—who happened to be around that weekend—read that last sentence out loud, a silence in which we seized up tight and looked around at one another with disgusted looks on our faces, and shook our heads. Another round of beer was ordered. Someone mentioned the phrase "class-action suit." There were property taxes to consider, at the very least. Imagine the sign at the city limits: Monarch, "The Morbid Village." Population: Less One. Someone dialed the mayor on his cell phone, but got only his answering machine. Lanahan Hopwith, a skinny used-car salesman with a big loaf of gelled hair, a cowboy hat and a drinking problem, said that if it were up to him, he'd saddle up and drive down to Manhattan on the spot, the faster to chuck rocks through that asshole reporter's windows! He then belched loudly and without embarrassment for a full five seconds.

In the end, we contented ourselves by agreeing that we would eventually write an angry letter to the editor, to be signed by the dozen or so of us there that night. A last round of beer sealed the evening. A final, stirring toast, and then we all filed out the door. The walk home alone was ten minutes of autumn starlight, purple distances, and crisp, thought-inducing air, and by the time I was on our front stoop I felt a small congratulatory upward lift to my feelings. Compared with most of the other people of Monarch, I had a good life and I knew it. Books and an occasional trip to Manhattan, a certain educated skepticism about the parade of facts as presented on our television and newspapers, and a passing knowledge of French, originally imbibed in high school and then maintained through an (deeply proud, I admit) airmail subscription to *Le Monde*. These things, along with a job managing an animal-research lab affiliated with the state university, and a certain detached if forgiving view of the operations of my own personality, added up to what Rob, I recalled, defined as "cultured." God, how he loved that word! In his version, it was the condition to which all intelligent life aspired. I should add that many people describe me as "taciturn." They often say I'm "close-mouthed." I've always resented the implied criticisms in these descriptions because—to myself anyway—I'm among the most interesting and dynamic people I know. A silence came toward me as I opened the front door of the house, an enveloping hush that told me the kids were already in bed.

"How'd it go?" Lucy was sitting at the kitchen table reading a novel. "The usual suspects?"

"I'm afraid so."

I placed my jacket on a kitchen chair and headed toward the fridge. Inside the lit box, in a far corner, my dinner sat sweating on a plate under a sheet of plastic wrap. Wordlessly I removed it and set it on the table.

"Except for Lanahan Hopwith," I added, but she was already reabsorbed in her novel and did not look up. I said no more and calmly began to eat.

Because we married fairly young, Lucy and I, we ran out of things to say early on, and were quickly forced to develop an accommodation with the deep silence at the

heart of our relationship. I still remember the bewilderment, even embarrassment this caused at first—as if we'd
both believed that the world would provide enough interesting material for a lifetime of conversation, and when it
didn't, we were so surprised by the failure we quite literally
didn't know what to say. For that reason, among others, a
cranky period overcame the two of us in our midtwenties,
when along with our growing boredom we were faced with
the daily "work" of being together—work highlighted
by the fact that we were still young and still theoretically
interested in sex with other people. Deepening irritability
drove us into counseling, and not long after to arrang-
ing our schedules, as directed, so as to provide task-free
intervals of time for the finer conjugal affinities to take
root. We sat across from each other at the dinner table
compiling lists of our desired qualities in a life partner.
We traded diaries and dutifully declared our "uninflected
nonconditional" love for each other according to certain
specific protocols recommended by a book published in
San Francisco. Once, out of curiosity, we visited a "swing-
ers' club" in Manhattan, but found the operations of
unbridled eros so depressing that we rushed back home to
our city on a hill chastened and with the feeling that the
long forked flames of the devil himself were pursuing our
car up Route 17. Then, as we grew older, the advent of
children seemed to throw a heavy tackle on our wayward
impulses. We now had a reason and a cause to have little
interest in each other, and that newly high-minded understanding made us tender together instead of confrontational. In the process, things between us became simpler,
more binary. Was it good for the children, or bad? Odd to

think of these two rosy-cheeked boys as marital transducers, swapping messages between their loving if otherwise snowed-in parents, but that, in essence, and among other things, is exactly what they are.

I ate in silence, reading the local paper. For several weeks after his death, Rob Castor news had continued to dominate the local headlines, and in a strange way, this continuity had been a comfort. There was a piecemeal sense of his presence lingering on in the announcement that a trust fund was being set up in his name; that a college scholarship was being established. Many towns would have buried and forgotten a local murderer as quickly as possible, but we individual citizens took a rugged pride in our fallen son, an in-your-face feeling of defiance about honoring him, stains and all, which, I had to admit, made me proud.

"Are you coming to bed?" Lucy was standing at the entrance to the living room, the novel open on her forearm, looking tiredly over my head.

"I'll be along, honey."

It was Friday night, the night, as it turns out, of our weekly scheduled sexual appointment. This had been a strategy adopted several years earlier to keep the guttering flame of physical intimacy alive. We had jokingly called it TGIF for "Thank God I'm Fucking," but increasingly of late, it had deteriorated into something irritable and subdued. According to Lucy, this was entirely my fault. She accused me of being a "head dweller," living in my mind like those arboreal animals that never descend from the canopy of trees. On top of that, she believed Rob's death had set off in me a strange emotional contraction, and that this new wave of withdrawal had crept unopposed (by me) into the very heart of our marital bed.

I followed her up the stairs, assisting myself with some heavy pulls on the banister, and into the bedroom. I was feeling bloated from the beery evening and the beans-and-franks dinner. More than that, I was afflicted, perhaps due to lack of sleep and generally rattled nerves, with an unnaturally sharp visual image of the food, halfway on its journey to intestinal glop, circling in the turbid whirlpool of my gut. This visual bloat was worse than the physical. My penis, when I dropped my pants at the foot of the bed, hung at a dispiriting half-mast as if commenting ironically on the scheduled sexual itch in my brain.

Lucy meanwhile had taken off her clothes and gotten into bed, where she lay naked, calmly staring up at me from the command post of her body. She has a naturally trim figure, with long legs, slim breasts and the lovely curving feet of the ballet dancer she was when a teenager. I haven't exercised in seven years and have lately grown soft and potted. What women find attractive is one of the mysteries of the universe. For a moment I wanted to take her and possess her roughly, but the impulse quickly passed, short-circuited by fatigue. She was meanwhile continuing to stare at me quietly. Probably, given my lack of initiative, she was thinking of giving up on the evening. Or maybe she was itching for the alternate satisfaction of a cigarette. She'd only recently stopped smoking, and the truth was that in a certain real way, though I didn't smoke myself, I missed those cigarettes of hers almost as much as I imagined she did. Not for the moon smell of ash on her breath, but for that way in which the cigarette seemed to hold out hope that everything wasn't completely tucked in and tidy-nice in our lives; that the world as it spun in the orbital belt of days around our house wasn't as entirely stable and stain free as it seemed and might, in the end, still surprise us. I needed that ventilating ounce of transgression. I missed it.

With a deep breath, I moved toward her, willing myself hard.

She closed her eyes and spread her legs.

I pressed my dry lips on hers, and soon after, entered her from a million miles away. High over my body, behind the shut eyes of the laboring sexual animal, my mind quickly filled with a lovely image of fertile green grass, and above this grass, a flung baseball that seemed to hang for a moment in the air, plump and fruity, before accelerating into my mitt with an explosive thump! In my mind's eye my father, a young man, was tossing the ball with me. He was lithe and happy, the hair was thick on his head, he was in the vibrant spring of his life, and I was still so small a child as to be frankly amazed by the physical facts of the backyard universe: the green fountain of the weeping willow tree, the smell of the summer air, and the way the boatlike prow of the roof of our house steadily, silently interrupted the going by of the sky.

"Are you going to come, darling?" my wife asked quietly.

With a racking sigh, I loosed a small burning arrow from the center of my body, a muscled entreaty to life to give something back. Sometimes, when she was in a good mood, Lucy went along at the moment of my climax, participating with subtle inner orchestrations that allowed me a long, delicious flight into the vaulted recesses of her body. But tonight, my mind elsewhere, I had the distinct sense of an impulse balked and pinching upward from the root of my sex. The feeling was wordless, but no less specific for that. Silently disappointed, I gave her a peck on the cheek, then withdrew from her and went to wash up. My cramped orgasm was already sending tingling sad antlers through my nervous system, and promising a night of bad sleep ahead. When I came back from the bathroom, Lucy had returned to her previous position of lying on her back with empty eyes, staring at nothing in particular. The only difference was that she was now covered up to the chin with a sheet and there was a downward sadness in the lines around her mouth. Basic human gallantry dictated that so soon after lovemaking, inquiries be made. I was clearing my throat reluctantly to ask her what was wrong when she beat me to it.

In a fake-casual voice, staring at a spot in space two inches over my left ear, she said that Rob's sister, Belinda Castor, had called and left a message asking that I call her back. Then, in an eloquent slither of sheets, my wife, still bearing within her the seeds of my desire to outrun death and stamp my face on the body of love, rolled over away from me, and all the way to the other side of the world.

# chapter 6

WE'D GROWN UP TOGETHER, ME AND THE Castor kids. It was hard to explain to outsiders, but we were a troop of three, and we moved with the synchronized thought processes of dolphins, or geese. If there was a fort to build, Rob assigned the roles and Belinda and I, a year apart, sprang into action. When we leafed through his father's mildewed *National Geographic*s, it was always Rob who held forth with impromptu lectures on ritual scarring while Belinda stood off to one side with her shirt yanked up, doodling barred lines on her chest with lipstick. And back in that time before we knew what our bodies were, or how they worked, or had had them filled with the important fluids of adulthood, it was Belinda who turned somersaults naked on our lawn and showed us the deep, pleated mystery between her legs.

I called her back the next day, at a number in California. I was oddly nervous while dialing, as if there was something at stake I wasn't quite aware of.

She answered the phone with that same surge of positive emphasis I remembered, that sonic boom of a "Hello!" traveling down the line.

"Belinda, it's Nicky."

"Well, hey, Nicky," she said, her voice brightening with affection. "Thanks for calling me back."

"No thanks necessary," I said. "I've been dying to talk to you in a hundred ways recently, B. In fact, I can't believe I haven't seen you."

"I had my reasons for staying away."

"Of course you did."

There was a pause.

"So how are you, Belly?" I asked, slipping easily into her old nickname. At the age of sixteen, shyly, clumsily and finally lovingly, Belinda had become my "first." By then she already owned the reputation in certain quarters for being a slutty girl who liked to touch boy's unmentionables in the dark, but I always saw her in a different light, as someone radiantly hip, ennobled by membership in the utterly strange cool family across the street, and owning a far more detailed knowledge of Hermann Hesse than I'd ever have.

"How I'm doing," she said, "depends on who you talk to. My boyfriend thinks I'm in shock, my psychiatrist thinks I'm depressed, my roshi thinks it's actually a milestone in my personal spiritual development, my employer thinks I'm faking it, and as for me, well, I have no fucking idea."

Very carefully and thoughtfully, I said, "Jeez, Belinda."

"I was sure," she went on, "that I was okay, actually. I

didn't want all the hoopla and crap of the memorial services in New York, so I did something very private, all alone here, burning some clothes on a mountaintop and chanting some griefy old poetry. I felt fine for a few weeks. Then suddenly, last week, I was going through this scrapbook that I'd found—"

"Uh-oh."

"Right, and kaboom, big time, actually. It was like the sky fell in. Lots of weeping and hysterical stuff. Gnashing teeth and throwing things. I felt like I'd taken some kind of timed-release poison pill and it wouldn't stop working."

"That sounds reasonably awful," I said, using one of our favorite old high school phrases.

"Yeah, well, it was fucking terrible is what it was. In fact, still is. I'm calling you now because I've decided that I need to tie up loose ends. There's a bunch of stuff I have parked in a long-term storage place in Monarch that I want to take back with me to California. His stuff, some of it. I'm coming in next week. Can we meet? I could use the moral support."

"Yes," I said, before I even had a chance to think about it, "you bet."

"Great," she said, "that'll make me happy, Nick."

"Me too," I said, grown suddenly happy myself. After college, as if trying to get it right, we'd come back together yet again, for one last time. It was during that period when I'd moved back to Monarch and, instead of applying to grad schools to study vertebrate paleontology as expected, had followed Rob's lead and begun smoking too much pot, reading pop physics, and cultivating a newly detached superior persona. Belinda had meanwhile taken an expensive degree at a Seven Sisters school and then warehoused her Tod's and sundresses and returned home to her Monarch roots, singing in a local grunge band called the Cahoots, and raging against the machine while spending her parents' money. Our relationship had traced a perfect thermodynamic arc: in six months we'd burned away everything but memories and an odorless wisp of ash. After that, I lost touch with her, and heard only rumors—of substance abuse, of several attempts at resurrecting a career in rock and roll, and of a brief sighting of her hooked up, incredibly, with a wealthy older dentist.

"How's Lucy?" she now asked.

The question seemed a bit abrupt. "She's fine," I said, "just fine."

"That's good," she said, and then after a pause, "isn't it?"

Alone in my study, I smiled at the familiarly blunt swerve of the conversation. Social niceties had never been Belinda's forte. A bomb dropper by nature, she was blunt, confrontational and indifferent to the normative expectations of "chat." This drop-dead volatility was one of the things I'd always loved about the girl. We talked for another few minutes, and I found myself growing familiarly warm and expanded on the phone. By the time we hung up, we were both laughing hard. When I went out to the kitchen, Lucy was at the table, paging through a magazine, pretending to ignore me. The boys, playing in the backyard, were making the shrieking sounds of raptors diving on prey.

"I just spoke to Belinda," I said.

"Oh?" She raised her eyes at me over the magazine.

"Yeah. She's feeling pretty broken up, as you can imagine."

"Poor thing."

"I'm going to see her sometime next week."

Lucy put down the magazine.

"See her?" she asked.

"Yes, she's coming into town and we'll have a condolence cup of tea."

"Well, isn't that lovely," she said, and braced her hand on the magazine and began intently studying her fingers, "please give her my regards."

"I will."

"Is she still fat?"

"Honey, please."

"I never understood how one could be addicted to speed and still be overweight. Can you explain that?"

I sighed. "This is not helpful, Lucy."

"Helpful? Who said helpful? She's just so"—Lucy wrinkled her lips—"*yuuuch*, isn't she? Have yourself deloused after you see her, Nicky, and by the way, please keep her away from the boys."

I shook my head wearily. "Is this really necessary?" I said. "I mean do we have to be *quite* this juvenile?"

"I don't know," Lucy responded mysteriously, "do we?"

OVER THE NEXT FEW DAYS, MY WIFE CONTINUED TO be short with me, and aloof as well. When her pride is wounded, she tends to react in just this way: by growing spitefully correct, formal and self-contained. The dinners served with quivering punctuality accompanied by taut mealtime conversation on the issues of the day; the perfectly squared piles of my freshly laundered shirts; the rigid arrangements of the boys' toys—I know the drill well, in all its hollow normality. More than hollow, it's punitive at bottom. And it works. In fact, it kind of kills me. I suffer when Lucy is like this. I suffer because it hurts to be marginalized by my life partner, and also because her predicament—its fraughtness, its nerved aloneness—nearly cripples me with the force of my own sympathetic response (roped to my awareness that I've probably grown too lazy, stalled or self-involved to do much about it). This is part of my problem in life, generally, this passive overabundance of seeing-it-from-the-other-side. Lucy was threatened by Belinda's wildness, and the way it attacked the codes by which she'd tried to run her own life. But she'd be damned if she'd admit it. In the early phases of our marriage, I would have tried simply to say, Darling, it's quite obvious. You dislike her because she's a risk taker, a wild and untamed spirit and is utterly uninvested in those social arrangements you hold so dear, but I love you, so who cares?

But our years together have curbed my enthusiasm for these kinds of dramatic reconciliations. Besides, truth, at least marital truth, is curved, not straight. It's more easily reached through sidelong glances than the burning heartfelt stare. It responds to inference better than it does to blunt disclosure, and sometimes is happiest being tastefully buried in the backyard. Exhibit A: the few times I tried to suggest that it was normal to want to see the sister of a dear dead friend, and encouraged her, please, to talk to me about it, Lucy coldly, definitively changed the subject.

# chapter 7

MY WIFE! MY LIFE! WE'D MET IN SOPHOMORE year in college. She had high cheekbones, a fresh-banana smell, burning self-confidence, and at the moment I first clapped eyes on her, was turning to confide a secret to a friend in class while her small, exceedingly shapely hand rose to cover her mouth. I was nineteen and determined that my women acquaintances understand that it was interesting to be as socially awkward as I was, and that as part of that interestingness, they go to bed with me. Lucy never did at the time, though she did allow herself to become the other half of a platonic couple (us), seen everywhere together, the exact nature of whose friendship remained a tantalizing mystery to all but their very best friends.

The heart has its own road maps. For several years after college, while weaving in and out of our respective relationships, we stayed vaguely in touch, Lucy and I, and we did so not only out of the residual momentum of closeness that had first brought us together as undergrads, but because both of us, in a way, kept the other in some deep reserve space from which they functioned as both a comfort and a goad. I've often thought of Lucy in that period as something like those dreamy, mysterious planes that make up the Strategic Air Command. No one sees them; their exact whereabouts are a mystery, but the fact of them, even abstractly, gives (or used to) a certain undeniable comfort to worried minds.

When we met again, I can't remember who it was who called whom to set things up. What I do remember is that we went to several dinners together, and that from the start we experienced the slightly buzzy, overly loud self-conscious feeling between us as pleasure. Everything we said seemed not only funny, but effortlessly to signal both back in time and reach forward into the future as well. This sense of continuity felt like a unique accomplishment, and if there was real ease when we finally fell into each other's arms, there was a touch of relief as well—relief at the thought that the entire humiliating audition of running to and fro in the world with your heart in a lockbox, praying for a loving soul to find the key, was over.

We got married in a small church outside Monarch. The sun was in my eyes for most of the reception, held on the church lawn—a circumstance that may account for the fact that in many of the photos of the event I have the look of a man squinting as if in a certain disbelief at his own future. Rob, already in the first throes of fame, was my best man, and flew in for the event from a West Coast writers' conference wearing his standard-issue bandanna, boots and vaguely Confucian scraggle-beard. Lucy and I had drawn up our own vows, and the service proceeded smoothly. It was halfway through dinner that things began to take a turn. As I'd somewhat both dreaded and keenly anticipated, Rob (who had been drinking Scotch like tap water since his arrival) got to his feet, cleared his throat, and began clinking his fork against his glass for silence.

"Ladies and gents," he said, when the room finally fell quiet, "I'm here to give away Master Nick Framingham, to whom I've owed money, love and life for two decades now. Nick's my oldest friend, aren't you, Nick?"

A scatter of indulgent laughter met these opening remarks. Feeling light-headed in my rented tux, I nodded warily. My parents, whose own relationship with Rob was one of alternating suspicion and warmth, did their best, by way of propitiation, to smile.

"Nick is now tying the knot," Rob went on, and I noticed his entire body shifting slightly forward and then back like a freighter caught in the steady, rolling motion of the sea. "The phrase 'tying the knot' would seem to refer to the closing off of something. It could mean, for example, torniqueting off a flowing vein. If that were the case," he finished pitched slightly forward, "that vein would probably finish somewhere near the heart of my sister."

There was a single snort of laughter from somewhere in the room, which seemed mainly to underline the sudden silence. In the tradition of best-man speeches, Rob was clearly determined to give me a good razzing. As for Belinda, she'd refused the event entirely, and hadn't even responded to the wedding invitation. In that, there was little surprise. Over the last years since our extended post-college fling, she'd been completely silent, indifferent to both my occasional phone calls and heartfelt letters.

"Just look at the man," Rob said, putting his glass down and waving a meaty hand in my direction. "Behold the groom!" I was beginning to feel distinctly ill at ease. "Nicholas Framingham is not a homosexual, that's the first thing to remember. He's merely got what the Buddhists call a mild heart."

An unhappy mutter coursed through the room. "Mainly what I want to say"—Rob drew himself up, seemed to recover his self-control suddenly—"is that we're here to celebrate love. Love!" he cried. "The immortal binder of human souls! Nick's soul called out across the fields and meadows of the world like a baying hound. Arf arf! And the beautiful Lucy's soul responded with its birdlike tweet tweet!" I thought I saw a large, balding member of Lucy's family getting to his feet, shaking his head. "At such moments as these, my friends, when the cup of life runneth over, let us remember the words of the blessed Chekhov, who said, and I quote, 'Don't get married if you're afraid of loneliness.'"

The balding man was now striding toward the stage. Rob, seemingly moved by his own speechifying, clasped his hands to his chest as if in supplication, and cried, "All I really want the world to know is that I love you, man! I just love you with all my broken heart! You're the best"—he seemed to take a swing at some invisible tormentor—"so, hey, *l'chaim!*" he cried. "*Sláinte, cincin,* bottoms up, baby, because . . ."

He leaned forward in the manner of sober diagnosis and added, "It's all downhill from here."

He sat down to the sound of Mac, and Mac alone, clapping loudly.

A YEAR LATER, WITH LUCY PREGNANT WITH OUR first child, Belinda passed through town. The two of them had first met each other years earlier, in my college dorm room, when Belinda came calling one weekend, and had loathed each other on the spot. Now Belinda showed up at our house for a "drink" and made a point of being perfunctory with my then-blooming, gorgeous wife. In fact, during the entire visit, in which she drank a whole bottle of wine while retailing—because I'd asked— stories about Rob, she seemed to be smothering a laugh of some sort, a high-handed snigger. Without ever saying anything, she managed to make Lucy furious, and we had a terrible fight in the wake of her departure. Two years afterward, with Lucy pregnant again, the same scenario ensued. "Why does she hate me so?" Lucy cried when she left. "And why do you let her near me?" In her mind their enmity was something archaic, even tribal, a mystical symbol-war fought with real feelings.

I didn't want Lucy hurt, and in the aftermath of that second visit, I swore to myself I'd never see Belinda again. But as the passions of the marriage rapidly cooled and settled, helped in part by the wonderful, indispensable, eros-shattering advent of children, I began to reconsider. Belinda, after all, represented to me a unique path back to my original nourishing sense of myself. She was from a time when the wide-open frame of possibilities was not yet filled in with the deadening actuarial facts of adulthood. After the death of Rob, the choice became even starker. My heart might have ached to see Lucy at a disadvantage, but my soul had its own requirements, and among them was that I somehow, at any cost, keep a live connection with the only touchstone of those days that was left.

## chapter 8

"YOU'RE STARING AGAIN," SHE SAID.

"Am I?"

"You're doing that . . . thing again."

"I'm sorry, darling."

"How can you just sit there and stare out the window while I'm talking to you? Don't you know how that makes me feel?"

"You're right." I lowered my gaze, smiling on reflex, and noticed, with a shock, that she was wearing the enhancement of light makeup. On top of that, she'd prepared an extra-special lunch of my favorite cold cuts. Every few weeks, out of the swamp of our complacency, moments like these would arise in which one of us—usually Lucy, I admit—would make an effort to somehow reinvigorate our marriage. The boys were away on a playdate. She was shaking her head.

"I'm sorry," I repeated.

"Is it the usual?" she asked.

"What do you mean?"

"I think you know."

"Not at all. No, I was just thinking about . . ."

"Let me guess."

There was a pause. "So what if I was?" I said.

"Rob?" she asked.

"Yes."

When her voice next came, it was unnaturally calm and tender. "Is it nice where you are, Nick?" she asked. "Is it warm and friendly? Is that why you spend all your time there?"

"Lucy—"

"Because it has been," she went on, her voice sharpening, "six months since the man died, and that's enough, don't you think? I mean, that's really enough. I married a husband, not a tombstone, for crying out loud!" and with that, before I could say anything else, she got to her feet, spun on her heel and strode quickly away, leaving me the bitter consolation of marveling at how her slim, lovely body excited absolutely no interest in me at all.

That same night, after eating dinner amid the weirdly particular new zone heating of my life (in which torrid warmth flowed from the four-foot-high band of our children, and a foot higher, persistent chill reigned), I gave into temptation, climbed the stairs to the attic and drew down Rob's precious old annotated copy of *The Dancing Wu Li Masters*, studying his exclamation points and excited marginalia. I took out his old deck of Bicycle cards whose fans, cuts and shuffles he'd always claimed had informed his understanding of how to write, and riffled them slowly, remembering. I was in the grip of something, and incapable, it seemed, of resisting it. The next day, still in a nostalgic trance, I went to the town library after work and peered into our high school yearbook. High school yearbooks are always dress rehearsals of adult life, and as such invariably freighted with pathos of a sort. Ours, called *The Sundowner*, was no different.

Sitting in the cramped carrel, smiling fondly to myself and feeling only slightly foolish, I paged slowly through the old book, rowing my eyes over the small color head shots set in neat mortuary lines. As the individual frames flickered past my vision, it was nearly as if I were watching an old film, and then presently, my eyes moving faster, as if I were launched past the images themselves and suddenly into a deep, still focus on the past. At the far end of the corridor of the book, I beheld a day of afternoon sunshine and loosely stacked end-of-summer clouds. Below those clouds was a covert of curling brush, insulated from sight and sound. And in the dirt of that covert my twelve-year-old self squatted, grinning. As was nearly always the case in the warm summer days of childhood, Rob was next to me, sprawled on some fallen leaves, wearing a T-shirt and scuffed jeans that terminated in a pair of red sneakers. We were talking about whether or not Jeanie Locasio would let me see her seventh-grade breasts during the coming school year. They were vaunted breasts, universally admired, and even more than to touch them, I wanted somehow to be *incorporated* by them. Rob laughed at the thought, and his eyes, luxuriantly lashed and sky blue, blinked with slow, sensual beats before he grew serious and asked, "What do you think it must be like to have tits? I mean real ones, that just lean out onto the air, and everybody looks at?"

"I dunno," I said. "I never even thought about it."

He rolled over on his stomach.

"Or that milk pours out of them. Then what?"

I had been sitting on my heels in the leaves, and at this, lay all the way back onto the ground and extended my legs. We were then lying next to each other, facing in opposite directions. Through the tapering needles of the shrubs the sun was flinging dancing motes, trembling bars of light.

"Girls are awesome," I heard him say. "They're chariots, man. They're these beautiful genetic machines that carry the whole human race on their backs. I want to marry Lisa Staley."

"Do you?" I asked, unable to resist the sudden rush into consciousness of all the things that were awful about Lisa Staley, that were rankly offputting about Lisa Staley; that in my opinion would have disqualified Lisa Staley from ever even presuming she could be with someone like Rob: she had hair that sometimes clumped greasily together and paper white pimply skin; once I was certain I'd heard her fart. But all these small cavils were erased as if in a single wave by the fact that Lisa Staley, at age thirteen, was possessed of an ineffable cool so distinguished that, when around her, it made me feel like a basset hound. She had a vast following of girls who dressed like her and imitated her verbal mannerisms down to the last detail, and it was obvious that she would never have even spoken a word to me if not for Rob. Among the many other things I loved Rob for was the fact that he'd never, not once, brought this up.

"Why?" I asked. "Isn't she kinda gross?"

He swiveled around and put his face next to mine. He smiled, and placed his hand affectionately on my shoulder. Alone among the hip kids, he didn't care that I was so überdorky I was never called upon by the teachers, or even noticed by the girls. He didn't give a shit that I wasn't—like the rest of his friends—instantly, cascadingly witty on command. But I wanted him to tell me something just then. I wanted him to address that hidden fierceness I felt in his company, otherwise hidden to the world. His hand on my shoulder was meanwhile sending warmth outward from his palm. His glowing, foxy face was looking at me from up close, smiling. I smiled back, hopefully.

"Because Lisa Staley is a goddess," he said, "and I want to be her Zeus."

My smile fell, and I watched as, pressing downward on my shoulder, he slowly levered himself to his feet.

"And because," he added, "we've decided to run away together. I'm sick of taking grief from Mom and Pops. I've got some money saved, and we'll take a bus away from here. It'll be like incredibly cool. What's the matter, Nick?"

"Nothing," I lied, and then noticed he was standing in front of me with his hands in his pockets, shifting slightly back and forth on his heels. I got the reference. Two weeks earlier we'd seen the video of the movie *Badlands* together in his basement while drinking his dad's filched wine, and in the casual alpha-male insouciance of Martin Sheen had glimpsed a vision of a jaded God whom each of us, for slightly different reasons, found irresistible.

"On the run," he was saying, "things'll be easier. Lisa's

a go and we've got people across the country we can stay with." He made of his finger a pistol and pulled the trigger. "When needed," he said, adopting a British accent in recognition of our beloved *A Clockwork Orange*, "a little bit of the old ultravee will serve to gather cash."

"What about your bar mitzvah?" I asked sensibly. "Isn't that soon?"

"Empty rituals for empty minds," he said in a deep stage baritone. "Besides," he added, "if need be we can dress you like me and you can stand in for me. My parents are already half in love with you anyway. 'He's so quiet. He's so well behaved.' Yeah, just cough a lot up onstage and no one will notice you can't speak Jew."

I laughed at this, and then stopped as the vaguely thrilling idea of being him in public stole into my mind.

"So, you wanna come over for lunch?" he asked. "Belinda and Hi are still at camp."

I felt, suddenly, like murdering him and I didn't know why.

"Whatever."

We made our way back through the forest, and onto his back lawn. As we entered the house, I glimpsed his mother in the distance. She was wearing a clingy dress that gave what seemed to me a shockingly obvious picture of her body, and shoes that mixed puffs of fur with impalingly long heels.

"Hi, Nicky," she said, leaning downward and into my field of vision through a nimbus of citrus bathwater, "how's tricks?" I looked back at her with my special fake dead smile, feeling the chill of the air-conditioning against my teeth.

"Fine."

"That's good. You guys hungry?" She looked over my head at Rob, jerked her head toward the kitchen, pirouetted on a heel, and clattered off without saying anything more.

"Leftovers from last night's dinner party," Rob said to me as he opened the fridge door, "with state senator Schulman."

I gave a small head bob, mostly to myself, as if to indicate that dinners with state senator Schulman were a common occurrence in my life, even if, in truth, there had never, not even once, been such a thing as a "dinner party" at our house, where my father, an industrial chemist, and my mother, a registered nurse, gave always the impression of fighting a pitched war against the forces of scarcity and want. Food was for eating, or better yet, nutrition; it was attacked with profound sobriety and indifference to taste or design, and played its part in a larger ongoing object lesson taught daily by my parents and entitled The Difficulty of Life. A sense of incompletion sighed at me from the unpainted walls of my room; from the battered, dingy paint of our succession of turret-shaped cars; from the scuffed grass of our lawn, and the pinching hand-me-down clothes of my older brother. It seemed painfully obvious that to cross the street from our house to the Castor's was to change not only economic but life-expectation zones as well. I couldn't believe Rob didn't see this, or if he did, refrained from saying so. I wasn't about to be the one to tell him.

"Try these guys," said Rob, holding up a serving dish, "they have nuts in the center and bacon on top."

I picked at the food that, being cold, had a kind of congealed thick taste to it, while Rob explained in detail about his getaway plan. But I wasn't listening especially. I remained snagged on the difference between our lives. Where did his family, for example, get such verve, while mine seemed stalled in the drab flats of existence? That couldn't simply be a question of money. And why was there such a prickly edginess of feeling between the two moms? As regards Shirley Castor, my mother was jammed with neighborly good intention. In her eyes, Shirley was "refined." She was "classy." But I never understood why she cringed as she said these things, or why this otherwise depressed woman loaded such streaming, nearly hysterical emphasis into her comments.

"Are you listening, bro?" Rob was frowning.

"Of course I am."

"Really, then what was I just saying?"

I had no idea.

Smiling at me, shaking his head ruefully, he leaned across the table and slapped me hard across the face. Rob had always had a nasty little violent streak, at odds with his ironical detached-kid persona. At the core of him was an explosive kernel of rage. I was profoundly passive by nature, but when hit I became crazy, and he knew it. We flew at each other, and tumbled together to the ground, punching and grunting. We would end up breaking one of his mother's delft serving dishes and Rob, as a result, would receive a grounding that would last the entire weekend. Yet twenty-five years later, sitting in the carrel with the yearbook open, what I recalled most vividly of that end-of-summer afternoon was the slight, welcome shock of the palm of his hand against my skin.

It was now dusk. Janitors were crisscrossing the floors behind their mops, drawing a cage of shining lines on the dark linoleum. The building would be closing in a half hour. Ignoring the deepening evening, I remained sitting still while continuing the meditation on Rob, and on the strange, preordained difference between his sprawling confidence and my own cautious self-containment, and on his temper. Did I have a temper? I suppose everybody did, for that matter. But mine wasn't like Rob's, no. It wasn't like the thing that happened to him when he lost control and seemed to whiteout in a blaze of human fury. It wasn't like waterspouts, ball lightning, and those other weather phenomena that come from absolutely nowhere, roar into the middle of an apparently sunny day, strike with violent force, and shatter the unsuspecting world around them into little bits.

Shutting the yearbook and getting up to go, I remembered the place where that violent streak eventually took him. It began, during the last days of his life in China-town, when, somehow, incredibly, he contrived to get a gun. No one to this day knows how. A dark and oily little piece of menace, it was called a Rolf .38. The gun was in his pocket as he left his miserable rented room for the very last time on the morning of June twenty-third and took the subway uptown. Kate was still asleep when he let him-self into their apartment with his old key. It was just then seven A.M. Newspapers reported that it was eighty-nine degrees at that hour of the day. The air-conditioning was running, and so Kate hadn't heard the key turning in the front-door lock. But she heard the bedroom door itself open, because, according to reports, the hinges squeaked loudly. Forensic detectives would later deduce that by the time her eyes focused, he was already standing in front of her.

# PART TWO

# chapter 9

ROB WALKED TOWARD HER FROM THE BED-
room door, before stopping at the foot of the bed. That
much we can surmise. Seeing him appear before her first
thing in the morning, Kate doubtless greeted him calmly
and began to chat. The habit of calmness was deeply
ingrained in her, but she also would have quickly realized
the situation was dangerous, and that in such circumstances
it was important to keep talking, to keep time expanding,
to maintain the fiction that everything was tranquil, and
that the sight of your ex-lover entering your apartment at
dawn due to a key you'd never bothered to get back from
him and standing before you now unshaven, stinking, and
with a suspicious pistol-shaped bulge in his pocket, was
just another casual event in your day.

We know that three months had gone by since he'd
moved out of their apartment, shouting that she'd betrayed
him for "Mammon." In that period, she'd seen him only

once, for a drink at a bar. It was an evening that had ended badly, according to eyewitnesses, with Rob "raising his voice and pointing his finger a lot." She'd subsequently received three e-mails from him. These were later read out loud at the trial. The first, in its entirety, ran, "Cruelty is not a religion, even when practiced diligently and with faith." The second contained simply the word "darling" in the subject box and as message bore a repeating cascade of *x*'s and *o*'s. The third, sent not long before Rob's morning visit, had a video attachment of the ritual slaughter of a lamb by Indian Muslims. Accompanying the attachment were the simple words, "There will be consequences."

Kate always gave the impression of being as organized as a Filofax, and beneath whatever conversation she was able to make just then she was surely already calculating the percentages and working up a plan. As she got out of bed, that plan was already in place. In the summer heat, she slept without clothes, and the first part of her plan would have been to face Rob with the full-frontal effect of her nudity.

What was running through his mind just then as she came toward him, unafraid? What was he thinking as he looked into the eyes of the woman who had dropped him hard, grown successful and then stomped on the hurt by hooking up with the man who'd helped make her famous? In the tragedy of what followed, I think all of us were struck by the fact that no one ever talked about how much he loved her through it all; no one spoke about how deeply attached to her he was, or how he began to feel himself literally shrinking as her literary celebrity began to grow. Artists live powerfully in their own imaginations and sometimes have problems believing they actually exist. Most likely, as she grew more concretely successful, Rob felt himself becoming ever more physically insubstantial. Mostly likely, as he lay in his miserable Chinatown apartment day after day, hemmed in by four walls and the crash of the crazy city traffic, he felt himself leaving his own body inch by inch, dematerializing from the floor up. By this logic, he was finally driven less by the desire for vengeance than to save himself from quite literally disappearing off the earth.

He stood in front of her, blinking rapidly—a habit of his from childhood when under stress. It was 7:14 A.M. Three minutes had elapsed since his arrival. An elderly Hungarian woman, Mrs. Halasz, lived below. She testified that while sitting in her housecoat waiting for the coffee to brew, she'd heard heavy feet on the stairs, and then the squeaking of the joists in her ceiling, followed by silence. This was soon interrupted by the sudden squealing of chairs on the kitchen floor.

Something strange was happening. Having in the interim donned a cotton robe, Kate was sitting down at the kitchen table, and Rob was sitting across from her. Two cups of half-drunk coffee were later found. The logical deduction is that Kate had apparently gotten up to make them, and then sat down again.

Probably by now she had begun to relax somewhat. The sun was out, the day was brightening, and in the little yellow dell of the kitchen, a certain kind of cheer reigned. A radio, tuned to a classical station, now popped on automatically, as it did each morning at 7:15 A.M. At that particular hour of that particular day we know that

Bach's Brandenburg Concerto was playing. As the violins fiddled and rose and fell in emulation of the sound of the ocean, she sipped her coffee and watched for cues that would tell her what to do next. Below the comforting burr of her own voice as she spoke to Rob she was likely looking around the room, sizing it up for its lethal potential, perhaps considering the heavy ceramic mug on the table in front of her. In the right hands, after all, a kitchen is a nest of glittering weapons. But for the moment, at least, she did nothing.

Somewhere between the first and second cups of coffee, Rob laid out *his* plan. In his backpack he had brought a large blue-cloth ringed binder, one of those notebooks of grade school. It was filled with his slanting windblown penmanship, the words set down as if they might at any moment scatter in a gust of feeling. The notebook was labeled simply "You" and was authored by "Me." A star piece of evidence at the trial, exhibited in a cloudy plastic bag, the binder was more than three inches thick.

It was an almanac of crazed obsession. Some of us took to calling it "the Fatal Valentine." There were five pages of nicknames. There were four pages of anagrams of the words "Kate Pierce I love you." In a separate section entitled The Truth there were pages upon pages describing her face, at rest, when smiling, in orgasm, and a series of caressing sketches of individual features—the "auburn chutes" and "gorgeous proteinic swirls," of her hair, the "petty crimes" of her shoulders. Employing all his art with words, he'd drawn the moment of their first meeting in prose, haloing it with foreknowledge on both their parts. He'd transfigured their two difficult years together in Manhattan as "a glide in the park," and elevated their down-at-heels apartment into a "pagan temple of shabby chic."

Mrs. Halasz testified that for a good long time she heard a "singsong" sound coming from the floor above, and at least initially, we were mystified by what this might refer to. But then it slowly dawned on all of us. The old lady was overhearing the sound of Rob reading out loud. She was witnessing Rob using his literary gift to try to drill through the retaining wall of a woman's heart.

# chapter 10

ON THE DAY OF MY APPOINTMENT WITH
Belinda, I was both sad and excited. I had e-mailed the
office upon awakening that I'd be late that day for medi-
cal reasons, and had come down to breakfast in a good
mood. But the atmosphere of the kitchen that morning
was in the nature of a major reality check. Things weren't
simply hostile. Things, rather, were deeply and seemingly
irrevocably sedimented with resentment. There was a long
silence in the room as I stared at the soggy archipelago of
my raisin bran, suddenly fatigued and feeling the house
at that moment seeming to weigh on me with its literal
downward pressure of three repeating floors of furniture,
rugs, bedding and clothes. I slumped in my chair. The
silence lengthened. With startling autonomy, a car drove
by on the street outside. When I raised my eyes, Lucy was
looking at me from the sink.

"What?" I asked quietly.

"Oh, please," she said, and then turned away.

What I would have loved, just then, was to be extraordinarily busy. I would have loved to be under the tearing pressure of deadlines, throwing up great clouds of vocational guy-dust while shooting away in a roar of career wheel spin.

Instead, still in my undershirt, I watched her back as she puttered around the kitchen a moment, cleaning up. When she's angry, her torso becomes unnaturally rigid, and she seems to be made of two people, the upper part spearing stiffly upward, the lower part still lithe and desirable. I gazed at this fantastical figure, this wifely hippogriff, while finishing my cereal in silence (the boys had already left for school). Then I came to the decision that, though defeated by Lucy's recent refusal to engage, I would give it another shot. I got up, pushing my chair back with a loud squeal.

"They're forecasting an unseasonably warm day today," I said in my most affable voice. "Why don't we do something with the kids when I get home from work?"

"Well," she said to the sink, still keeping her back to me, "I can think of at least two reasons."

I crossed the room and went up behind her.

"Come on," I said softly, "this is crazy, honey. Lighten up."

"Why?" she asked the sink.

"You know why."

"No I don't."

"Because"—I waved my hands in the air, unseen by her—"there's nothing there."

She whirled around to face me, and put her hands on her hips.

"Nothing where?" she asked.

"Nothing between me and Belinda Castor," I said.

"Oh, Nick," she said, "Nick, my darling husband." She smiled pleasantly as she turned back to the sink. "Where was I exactly when you became so utterly full of shit?"

"She's an old friend, and that's all," I said, determined to ignore the provocation. "And you know how I've been lately, since everything that happened"—I waved my hands again—"with Rob. It's like, she's the only link in the world left back to the guy and I need to go there."

"She's my enemy," she said firmly, salting a sponge with Ajax. "And once upon a time that would have been enough for you."

I stared at the place where her hair began on the thrillingly long stalk of her neck and felt my heart begin to pound for reasons I couldn't understand. I massaged my forehead.

"Number one, that's ridiculous," I said, "And number two, I know she's not your favorite person, but I need to see her for me, *me*"—I raised my voice—"*I* need to see her, honey. This is exactly the kind of thing that will bring me some closure. And maybe the only thing."

"*Closure?*" She'd whirled around to face me again, and spoke slowly and loudly, as if rage had made her hard of hearing. "He was someone you knew from about a hundred years ago, Nick. We're not talking about a parent here. We're talking some circle-jerk buddy from childhood. I mean, look"—her shoulders suddenly fell—"sweetie, I know it hurt you that he died. It hurt me too, but just how pathetic is it that you're still whacked out about it, months later, and that you're going sniffing around his *totally* unstable sister to boot?"

"I'm not sniffing around her," I said, trying to kill the wobble in my voice. "She called. I called back. I'm going to see her for a couple hours. And by the way, I don't care if it seems pathetic. Pathetic is for other people. What *I'm* telling you is that I need to do this, that it's important to me, and that while I understand your dislike of the woman, I simply don't think it worth getting into a major meltdown over."

"And what I'm telling you," she responded instantly, "is that you're stealing from this marriage to service some Tom Sawyer fantasy about your past that never existed."

"Is that really for you to judge?" I asked.

She gave a short, bitter laugh. "Uh, yes," she said, turning to go, "it is." She started up the stairs, and after mounting two of them, stopped and turned back to where I still stood, my hands uneasily in my pockets, shaking my head at no one in particular.

"You're blowing it," she said, "you're blowing it, Nick, and you're gonna regret it." Another two stomps up the steps. "And remember to take out the recyclables today—it's paper day." A receding series of thumps as she stomped down the hall. "No, plastic, sorry," came the voice, trailing off as it entered the bedroom and was end-stopped, a moment later, by the sound of the door being slammed.

I got in the car in a strange, whirling mood of exhilaration and despair. Belinda had requested that I simply meet her at the storage facility rather than a coffee shop, and as I drove there, I found myself stabbing the gas and the brake, taking corners on the edge of traction, and arriving at the battered front office in a rush of slurring gravel. This was not eagerness; it was the familiar expedient of scapegoating the nearest thing at hand. When younger, a chain of broken toys, then busted go-karts, had performed the same service. I slammed the car door hard and then entered the office. The desk clerk told me that Belinda hadn't yet arrived, and I settled down to wait.

A quarter hour of paging through old *Newsweeks*, and I heard the snoring sound of a far-off car with a broken muffler. Presently this grew in volume to a roar, and preceded the arrival of a small dusty truck, which bounced over the rutted gravel of the parking lot and slewed to a stop. The shape of the driver's head told me it was her immediately. The truck door popped open, and as she got out, I received the strange impression of a person blurred by time but still instantly recognizable. Dressed in black and wearing a black bandanna pirate style on her head, she looked cute, big nosed, tired and definitely heavier than I remembered.

Belinda entered with a self-important rustle of clothes, and went up to the counter, not seeing me where I sat watching her over my magazine. In her low voice she gave the clerk her name and asked for the keys to a certain locker. While she waited, I stood up, fighting nerves, and went over and introduced myself. I had forgotten how intensely blue—like Rob's—were her eyes. Nearly instantly a shocked smile spread across her face. "Good lord!" she cried. "Have you been here the whole time? You look great. How are you, friend?"

"I'm fine, fine, Belinda. And what a—how nice it is to see you."

After a moment's hesitation, she leaned forward, delicately for a big girl, and put out her cheek to be kissed.

As I kissed her back, I was reached by a faint scent, a mix of female odors and long travel in a closed car, which I found oddly stimulating. Uncertain what to do suddenly, I coughed into a fist.

"And so?" she cried in a throaty voice.

"Ma'am?" The clerk, having waited for a lull, chose this moment to speak. "Would you sign this, please?"

She was still smiling as she reached down and doodled her signature, and then turned back to me.

"I'm stunned by how good you look, first of all," she said, and laughed again, with a big depth of lungs in the sound, in a way that reminded you, whether you liked it or not, of the power of her body.

Laughing along with her, and a bit struck by how unbereaved she seemed, I told her that marriage with kids meant no late nights and merely an occasional glass of wine, and the truth was that being bored was the best fountain of youth known to man. I found myself settling easily into this mode of deprecation of the thing—my marriage—I'd spent years painstakingly building from the ground up. She laughed again, holding my eye, and asked if I'd accompany her to her shed. We left the building, and as she walked to her pickup truck, she cast her eye at my dusty Chevy Suburban.

"Wow," she said, hopping into her truck, slamming her door behind her, and then leaning out the window, cheerful, "is that thing big enough for you?"

A minute later, we were pulling into parking places, and then she was getting out and standing a moment stretching while holding one hand in the small of her back. "Oh, these old bones," she said, and I laughed as I watched her lifted throat, creamy like a splash of milk against the black fabric, floating over the bending front of her body. She'd always been unembarrassed about her body, and I told myself, standing in front of her and having no choice but to look on as she flexed and groaned, cracking, that I now understood that perhaps she wasn't loose at all but rather simply indifferent to other people's opinions, and that this had been misinterpreted by the uptight high school tribes. Maybe I was simply guilty for how we'd first sawed at each other during that hot, throbbing summer of those many years ago, but I enjoyed reinterpreting her previous reputation in this new light. It made me feel good inside.

"You okay, Rollo?"

She was looking at me closely. Rollo was her pet name for me.

"Me?" I said. "I'm great, B. I'd be lying if I said I wasn't *very* happy to see you, but I'm fine."

"Me too. I only ask because you're looking a little pale there," she said, and yawned with a waft of stale bacterial breath. "Whaddya say we check out the storage?"

We shrugged open the garage door to the unit, and then poked around amid the old piles of furniture, and the tarped-over mysterious lumps and the things tied with batlike folds of fabric. "I didn't know Dracula lived this far north," I said, clearing the way.

She laughed.

"Speaking of which, I recently saw your mom on a condolence call." I hefted a large dusty candelabra that looked like a huge knobbed hand and examined it. "Her house is kinda dark, you could say."

"Dark? The woman lives like a refugee in her own home.

Once or twice a year I whisper the phrase 'managed care' in her ear and she doesn't talk to me for a month. Lemme guess, she was blotto."

"Uh, yes she was, I'm afraid."

She shook her head to herself and sighed. "It's hard to get her to stop the one thing left that gives her any pleasure. I really do appreciate you going, Nick. You always were the little gentleman"—she picked up an antique iron and blew dust off it—"and I'm sure it meant a lot. Do you think this thing is worth something?"

Looking at her, delighted with the quick pivots of her conversation—her speech rhythms were clearly those of someone who'd spent years away from Monarch—I told her that there was a new antiques store in town, and maybe she could get it evaluated there. She said nothing, and into that silence I suddenly found myself talking rapidly, for some reason. I could feel the cursive shapes my lips and mouth made as I gave a little speech about how the town had changed, and how the people had changed with it, and about the new crop of parents, of which I was one. I could hear myself babbling on robotically about the real but difficult satisfactions of home life, and how, though for a while things had been rocky between Lucy and me, we seemed to have found our own real if somewhat fragile peace. I liked that peace, I said, lying. Belinda wasn't speaking back. She seemed instead to be wholly absorbed in staring at her iron. Finally she put the iron down.

"Come here," she said, and when I took a step forward, still talking, she bent over and kissed me on the mouth. Her lips were covered with a faintly waxy paste that tasted of synthetic fruit, but behind that was a deep, roused plumpness that dropped through my body in a hot curtain. The arches of my feet curled.

"Relax," she said softly.

I was too flustered to speak for a moment.

"You're with an old friend who knows you very well. I don't need the blow-by-blow of the last ten years. It means a lot that you came to see me today, Nicky. It's important for me and I thank you for it."

I looked at her, feeling static and suddenly expanded within at the same time. It was one of those bell-timbre moments. I think I began smiling stupidly.

"You're welcome," I said.

She laughed at me, but gently, and in a way that was so familiar to me it was like a touch upon the foundations of my own soul. Even the silence that followed seemed familiar. During that special high school summer twenty years earlier, we'd been apprentice dharma bums together, transported by the dreamy mumblings of Carlos Castaneda to a place where we found the quiet itself a fraught, richly communicating thing. If we listened carefully enough, we were certain that the distances had a hiss; that trees sighed, even on windless days; that clouds breathed their way backward across the sky. In that bell jar of sacred silence, we slowly took off each other's clothes, and fucked votively, struck dumb with reverence for the way quiet seemed naturally to gather around our moving bodies. I couldn't help smiling as I remembered the innocence of that summer, and the way we dressed throbbing desire in high-toned sentiments. Later, after college, it would all become much easier. I lifted my eyes and looked at her. A wall of ancient feeling stood between us in the dusty air of the shed. She leaned forward through the wall and threaded her fingers into mine.

"This is nice," she said quietly.

"Yes it is."

We looked away from each other, both embarrassed, I think, by the sudden surge of feeling, and then she gently unlaced her hand from mine, and we continued to move through the things, but more quietly, she sorting what she didn't want into one pile of junk, and taking those few pieces—an antique sconce, some candlesticks, a beautiful pewter serving set—she did. After about half an hour, we were done.

"So hey," I said impulsively as she pulled the squealing garage door back down.

"What's that?" She turned to me.

"You wanna come out with me to Padi-Cakes for a snack or a drink or something?"

She laced her arm in mine. "You bet," she said.

For several years now, Padi-Cakes has been the only place in Monarch where I feel myself somehow lofted out of the town entirely. Rich hippies moving up here from Manhattan a few years ago styled the place on an Indian teahouse, with high arches and lots of fancy colored tile like an explosion in a Chiclets factory, and the visuals, along with the wheedling drone music, tend to carry the mind far away.

"You've changed," she said, as we began the process of loading the stuff into the back compartment of her truck. "You seem, I don't know . . ."

"Older?"

I could hear the sound of a smile in her voice as she walked behind me and said, "No, more at peace, I think."

We finished loading and I offered her a ride to the restaurant in my car. She accepted, and as we drove, I continued to try to banter with her, but she was flowing into a new channel. She stared out the window, saying little, responding with small phrases when necessary. Now that the initial excitement of seeing me had settled a bit, she was slowing, sobering, growing more reflective. When we got to the restaurant, I parked and shut off the engine, but made no move to get out. She for her part simply continued to sit there, saying nothing. After a long moment, she lowered her head. Gently, very consolingly, I placed my hand on her knee.

"Yup," she said simply.

"I know," I said.

There was another long silence.

"It's not," she said quietly, "that I simply miss him like a kind of sickness, Nick, or that I think about him constantly, or whatever. It's the *awayness* of it that I'm having trouble with . . ."

"Of course it is, Belly."

"It's like on a basic physical level, I just refuse the whole thing. I mean, the body that was there, vivid, so powerful—it couldn't just go away, could it? I keep feeling there's gotta be some way back. I keep feeling it's like he's in the next room, and can't figure out how to turn the door handle and get back in. I can hear that rattling handle in my dreams. I can't believe he's never again gonna call me drunk from jail in Laredo, Texas, or all bent out of shape about some new Finnish poet he just read, or harangue perfect strangers in bars about sustainable planetary resources. I can't believe we'll never ever have another chat about"—she pronounced the word with self-conscious pride, smiling a little—"Pantisocracy."

"What's that?" I asked.

The smile trembled. "One of those pipe-dream nineteenth-century English utopias he loved so much. The British, he used to say, were into utopias because the Industrial Revolution had driven them fucking crazy, every one of them, and being an island race, the only place they could go was back in time. Nostalgia and bad teeth, he used to say, are the British vices."

"And drinking."

"Whatever."

"You love quoting him."

"It's what I've got left." Her face drew down around the mouth as she stared out the window, and then slowly shook her head, mostly to herself, and said in a low voice, "Everybody thinks they have to say something to me. But none of it helps. Nothing does, actually. Not a single thing." She continued to look out the window, and then slowly turned to me. "And here we are with all our shitty old memories, eh, Nick?"

"He loved you very much," I said softly.

"Ah, Christ!" She shook her head, and then cried emphatically, "That fucker!" She wiped her eyes roughly with the back of a hand. "That goddamn golden little fucker! We all fell in love with him, didn't we, Nick?"

"We sure did," I laughed, "and he made a point of it."

"You know I once took an abnormal psych course," she said, "and I learned that there's this thing, this syndrome,

that happens if you grow up in a home with a handicapped child, in which the afflicted kid becomes the sun
of the family galaxy, and everybody else rotates around
him about a million miles away in space. Well, it was sort
of like that in our family. But there was no handicapped
child. Guess what we had instead?"

"Would that be an older brother?"

"A prince of the motherfucking realm. And me and
Hiram? We watched. Oh, yeah, we were big watchers. That
was the idea, apparently. My mother had him to dote on,
and us to be the audience. 'Here you go, darling,'" she said
in a mincing mother's voice. "'That's a good girl, swallow
it down to the really bitter part. Now take your sorry,
skulking useless ass out to the living room and watch your
older brother play the piano. Watch him win the state
spelling bee. Watch him be the shortest kid in town history to dunk a basketball!' God, it was never ending!"

As I watched, she seemed to shake her head as if somehow in censure of her own memories. Then she calmed
herself by doing what I took to be a yoga exercise, shutting
her eyes, straightening her spine, and breathing deeply, in
then out.

"By the way, what did she say to you when you went to
see her?" she asked a few moments later, opening her eyes.

"Your mom?"

"Yeah."

I shrugged my shoulders. "Oh, you know, the usual,
about missing Rob, as you'd expect, and the specialness of
it all; the love between them and stuff like that. She seemed
to take Hi's agronomy career as a personal betrayal—"

Belinda snorted.

"I know," I went on, "and of course there was the usual bit about what a tragic mistake it was to move to Monarch in the first place from San Francisco. Oh, and seals."

"Of course"—she was nodding—"and sea fog. Did she mention sea fog?"

I laughed. "And sea fog as well."

There was a pause.

"Nicky?"

"Yup."

"Did she say anything about me?"

I took a long, blind perusal of the view, considering what to say, and then decided to tell her the truth.

"No."

She nodded. "I can't say it surprises me."

"I'm sorry."

There was a sustained silence. And it was then, finally, that Belinda began to cry. There was no intermediate step of gradually gathering congestion. She simply made a sudden plosive sound of release and abruptly, with no warning, started sobbing out loud. On instinct, I put my arms around her and gathered her toward me. "That bitch!" she gasped, and then she buried her face in my neck, and sent fishlike flurries of grief through my clavicle and upper chest. "Why did I know that?" she kept repeating. "Why did I have to be so sure about that? Couldn't I be surprised for once in my fucking life?"

Petting her hair comfortingly, I held her as best I could and told her that I was there for her, that her mom was an old and unhappy alcoholic, that we would get through the difficulty of Rob together, that I couldn't believe what a deep and real and righteous feeling it was to see her again, and then, spontaneously, I told her that I'd missed her. I told her that I'd missed her friendship and our companionship. I don't know if she even heard me, because she was crying openly now, with breathless cycling little sobs. We stayed that way for a long while, me holding her, she bent forward into the windbreak of my chest, her sobs gradually slowing to sniffles, and then from there slowing further still. I was still talking softly when she turned her face toward mine and I had a chance to glimpse the pretty starbursts her matted eyelashes made around her blue eyes before we began to kiss.

## chapter 11

It was as if, from the very beginning of my life, the deepest lessons offered me were to squelch my own desires and swallow the taste of my feelings in silence. The point, my parents seemed to imply through their words and actions, was not to offend, or in any way draw attention to one's self, not out of adherence to some larger code of gentlemanly conduct, but because life itself was a highly breakable object, and as such must be approached sidelong and with the maximum caution.

That being the case, it's little surprise that my mother and father never seemed particularly to care whether or not I was happy as a child. They did the necessary amount to sustain, clothe and feed me, but I never felt that easy, lifted sense I perceived in the homes of my friends, whose families were organized around them so as to place them on pedestals of loving attention. No such elevation ever took place for me in our home. And yet, from as far back as I remember, my older brother, Patrick, seemed to dwell within a different world entirely, a world of parental recognitions, ecstatically applied. Their voices were more vibrant around him, the laughter more frequent, deep and sustained. I used to wonder if it wasn't simply that he, Patrick, had received the family's feelings firsthand, with the result that by the time they got to me, their freshness had been wilted by sustained handling, like old salad.

Much of this withheld feeling I attach to my father. In memory, it's as if he passed my entire childhood silently seated at the dinner table with his hands templed together over his nose, his eyes suspended and seeming to float in space while he stared at me in a grave, faintly accusing way. That same pinched face is a constant in an otherwise whirling array of recollection, and I can shuffle these images like a deck of cards. Here he is at the annual Christmas party for his lab, morose among the noisemakers and confetti poppers, with me trailing behind him, grabbing his coattails, attacked by shyness. Here we are all together on vacation, sitting becalmed in a sailboat in the middle of an Adirondack lake, or grimly eating in the campus cafeteria on parents' day at college, or sitting on a Connecticut beach avoiding looking at one another with the crumbling, hissing folds of waves a distance off. At the center of it is that remarkable document, his face, from which, in memory, a radiant dourness seems to emanate a little like the sunlit rays around the pyramid on the back of the dollar bill.

Why, I often wondered, did he begrudge me the happiness of my boyhood? Why was he so unalterably opposed to my joy? There is a sound recording that exists of me as a six-year-old child. I listened to it not long ago. On the tape my voice can be heard breaking upward in little interrogative crests. Those crests—I remember them well—were so many entreaties that my father join me in the excitement of childhood; they were my implicit request that he play with me with the ease and amplitude he did with my brother, Patrick, and that we be, if even for a moment, like those other fathers I saw at school, who seemed to exist with their sons in a quiet trance of understanding, letting their arms fall casually across their shoulders, building Pinewood Derby cars with them in long hours of basement collaboration, or camping with them in the nearby sawtooth mountains and thereby opening up vistas of manly expertise. I wanted the dashing fathers of the Italian kids; I wanted the terrible drinking fathers of the Polish kids. I wanted anyone who would hold his son in the safe boxed enclosure of a fatherly embrace. But my own father, though he knew that I'd clumsily fished for his approval for years, and knew as well that I was in love with the vast, cold competence with which he moved through life—my father simply sat before me throughout my childhood, as still as an Indian brave, the disembodied eyes floating in space, refusing to unbend an inch.

And now, here, I'd like to talk of one particular night of our family history. I'd like to dwell on an evening of childhood summer during that time of late August when the earth gives the impression of having slowed to a crawl in its orbit and standing ghosts of heat mist hover beneath the trees. I'd like to concentrate a moment on the three of us, mother, father and myself, in the kitchen waiting for Patrick to return on his bicycle. My mother is at the stove amid her chiming pots and pans, and seated at the table, I am attempting, as usual, to find such watercourses of enthusiasm as move beneath the dry surface of my father's disconnect. Should I try magnetism tonight? Or the truth about the curve ball? Will it be Brownian motion, which makes the blue of the sky blue, or *The Chemical History of a Candle*, by Michael Faraday, which I've lately read and been stunned by? Intuitively, I'm sure, I've opened one of those subjects of science or physics about which my father can grudgingly be convinced to trickle out small explanations. Probably, almost certainly, I am rapt. It is then that we become suddenly aware of a disturbance in one corner of our peripheral vision. Appearing at the screen door, which has been left open because it is the 1970s and nothing bad will ever happen, is a man-size shadow. The shadow, we presently realize, is a familiar form, and it is struggling to say something. It is Marc Castor. I know of my father's especial scorn for Marc Castor. He refers to him as a "clotheshorse," and a "goofball." He looks at him whenever the two men are in the same room, with a parched disdain. I've never understood his enmity toward a man who has always taken such pains to make me feel welcome in his presence. Tonight he has done the rare thing of showing up at our front door, which he's almost never done before. Also it's as if he's dancing under the influence of some strange music. He is thrashing his hands and waving his head back and forth. It looks a little like the Twist. Suddenly we understand his words.

"It's Patrick!" Marc is shouting. "He was hit by a car and the ambulance is coming! Come quick now migod!"

Then he stops, and merely stands there, his hands held up in the air, swaying.

That's the scene, and it stays that way no matter how many times I replay it in my head: the three of us frozen in our places by news that is already bursting over us like a shell, and yet in memory forever still in the pre-ground of that tragedy, forever still on the near side of all that consequence, and for those slender few instants that remain, still a family comfortably upheld by having dodged so many of the unhappy outcomes of life. I watch our faces fall open in surprise as a pulsing, sirenlike wail starts to pour from my mother's mouth.

Can anguish change the shape of a life? The car, as it turns out, had crushed Patrick's skull. It hit him broadside, moving fast, and flung him high through the air and onto a lawn. Marks on his face of a vaguely crosshatched pattern were later revealed to be the impress of the grill on his flesh. He lingered perfectly still in a coma for several days, then opened his eyes, made a small tasting movement of the lips as if in receipt of some new, not especially good information, and died. With his death, time stopped as it does when the projector jams at the theater and the handsome figures on the screen freeze and are cruelly lacerated by giant widening holes. The cleaning lady stopped coming. I no longer went to band practice. Inside the house there was no radio, no television, no sound at all for days save the surprisingly deep, masculine noises of my mother's grief as they drifted from the bedroom, and those of my father, who sobbed out loud in front of me and didn't care if I saw. But I did care. And it tore me up, hugely. I sobbed along with him, but I wasn't crying only for my brother. I was also crying because I was shocked that the one untouchable thing in my life—my father's feelings—had been hit that hard, and not for me.

In the days after the funeral, I spent a lot of time visiting compulsively with my brother's orphaned keepsakes and toys. It wasn't only that his baseball mitt, his little tin trophies, his white plastic flute, his gem collection, his train set, his plastic soldiers and his three-quarter-size Colt revolver reminded me of him. It was that his sudden death had turned these possessions directional. They continued to move ahead in time as if there was a lag between this world and the next, and the news hadn't yet reached them of their owner's death, and in the meantime, stranded between worlds, they must continue to carry on as plucky little bits of metal and plastic and leather waiting for a human touch to set them to life. Maybe that's why, when no one was watching, I crept into his room and held them individually in my hands for hours at a time, staring at them like you might a bunch of baby rabbits discovered magically unharmed beneath the blades while mowing the lawn, and said strange, impulsive things to them, day after day, which made me feel better.

Two weeks after Patrick's death, another school year began, with its social gates and enclosures, its rigid stratifications and its shaming categories: geek, dork, pussy, nerd. I was disoriented by all the feeling recently blown through our family, and dreading as well the reckoning that the beginning of a school year seemed to provide. And yet help, as so often in that period of my life, arrived in the providential form of—who else—Rob.

Utterly indifferent to the social price he was paying, he seemed to have grown even more attached to me than before. It was as if my friend were determined to fill the hole left behind by Patrick's passing and to surround me in a gated enclosure of warmth and attention. "I love you, Nick," he told me, whenever he had the chance. He said it in complete indifference to the snickering classmates, the occasionally askance look from homeroom teachers and head-shaking janitors. "I love you, guy, and you're just a champ for how well you're doing," he'd say, with that reckless, heart-flooded way of his. As time went on, however, I gradually came to understand that there was more than just simple affection in Rob's new flare of interest. In the aftermath of my brother's death, he was convinced I was now the possessor of "special information."

"You know," he asked me one day, "that brothers have all sorts of duplicate genetic matter and psychic overlaps, don't you?"

"Sure," I said.

"Well, so—and forgive me very much for asking—but I guess my first question is, like, at the moment he died, did you feel anything special? Did you like feel a pain in your body where the car had hit him, or get suddenly sad, or when you stood up did you realize you were bleeding from the nose?"

We were sitting that afternoon in our brushy covert sanctuary, as usual. His eyes were hot with excitement, and he was leaning toward me, blinking rapidly in expectation. I wanted above all to make him happy, and so the lie came easily.

"How'd you know?" I asked.

"Because I know, don't worry how."

"Well, it did. And it was kinda incredible. It was like I was just sitting there reading a book, and suddenly I grew all light, like I was floating. I felt this kind of pointy thing coming off the top of my head, like my brain was trying to get somewhere." I looked at him seriously, waiting a beat. "At the moment Patrick died, the pointy thing on my head shot through the window and never came back."

There was a moment of awed silence. "Oh, man," he said softly, "I mean," he went on, "*oh, man*. You see, that's exactly what I'm talking about. You know stuff. You've got, like, access to things that people would kill to have. We should form a death club, you know, and read von Däniken and shit and get a Ouija board and make contact. Everybody's got some kind of story to tell. After my gran croaked I was certain she was hanging out under the stove for about a week. Listen, have you ever huffed?"

"Huffed?" I asked. "What is huffed?"

"Like, making yourself nearly die and then coming back."

"I don't think so."

"Wanna try it?"

"Okay," I said reluctantly, not liking the sound of it but wanting to play along.

"Great, stand up."

I got to my feet.

"Now deep breathe," he said as I began to take long swimmer's breaths.

"Faster."

I quickened the rhythm.

"Now go faster, guy."

I was panting hard as he shouted, "Okay, stop, and

hold it!" and then came up behind me, snugged me into an embrace, and began, ever so gently, to choke me with a modified headlock. The crook of his elbow was cutting off my windpipe, but he was doing so with a kind of loving roughness that caused a wave of heat to rush upward from the middle of my chest and burst with a giant fissioning bloom of white in my head. For a long moment, I felt grown long and thin, as if streaming free of my body and tethered only by a wispy tendril of nerve. Then my chest swung open and I fell out of myself to my hands and knees, and then continued falling rapidly toward the hot, heavy center of the earth. My flesh buzzed on my bones, and just before I passed out, I had time to note that I felt weirdly naked beneath my clothes, and helpless, and I liked it.

Six months after Patrick's death his room was repapered and hung with new curtains and carpets. A gigantic television was installed where his bed had been, and my father, mainly, sat staring at it blankly on evenings and weekends. As for me, many years later, having long ago stopped thinking about my brother, I found myself strangely sensitive to the way in which his features would show up in other people. I once felt instantly at home with a gas station attendant because he had my brother's nose, and for a moment hungrily probed his background in a way I would realize only later was a groping on my part toward an old, flickering pulse of feeling. I was unnaturally warm with an elderly woman who picked at the corner of her mouth with her pinkie like my brother did, or sneezed with his funny little ladylike report, or I would notice how the shape of someone's head precisely mimicked what I had always thought of as his, and would sidle up to that person at a party, and speak with inappropriate candor out of the feeling that we were part of some larger conspiracy dedicated to keeping an old memory alive.

My dear, dead, freckled brother!

# chapter 12

LUCY WAS WAITING FOR ME AT HOME WHEN I returned from work looking like a blacked-out city. I swept into the house and saw her standing in the living room purposely dressed down in frumpy dark clothes, her face shuttered tight and her arms held at her sides. Not a photon of light would escape from that crunched mouth, those lowered eyes. And though I greeted her cheerfully where she stood, brushing past her with a breezy remark about the delicious cooking smells in the air, she sent the clear signal that the best thing possible, from her point of view, was that I leave her alone. If I could somehow cease to exist in the process, so much the better.

It had been two days since my afternoon with Belinda, and during that time Lucy and I had exchanged little more than the bare minimum necessary to sustain life. It was suddenly like being married to a swiveling, woman-size plate of green aquarium glass. From behind that glass,

I could watch the word bubbles drift upward from her mouth. I could see her fingers splayed slightly against the clear surface in greeting or good-bye. But all I heard was the faint, underwater hiss of her breathing.

During dinner that night, I remained extra animated, with the children especially, and I tried to catch a variety of small ripples of momentum from the boys upon which to float my way across the table and touch her with warmth. I was an old hand at this kind of redistribution of feeling, this sneaky intergenerational transfer. But on this night, as on the previous few, it was no dice. She was as skillful as I was at maintaining an open channel with the boys while keeping me out in the cold, and though I admired her virtuosity, the anaerobic withdrawal of feeling stung me.

All of this was especially sad because, buoyed by my transgression—a half hour of making out with Belinda in the car; an hour of excited chat in the restaurant—I was not only tactically happy, I *was* happy. I felt renewed in my marriage and I wanted her to know it. Pity is a vasodilator of the heart, just like love. And yet it's not love, for it requires a loss of some sort to activate it. Lucy, without knowing it, had lost ground and become an object of my pity. And I, without understanding why, had felt the charge of that emotion and pronounced myself newly in love.

Over the next few days, I continued to observe my wife with fresh eyes, noting as if for the first time the bending grace of her figure, her gentleness and kindness with the children; her diligence in running a house whose cleanliness and order I had always taken for granted. Uncomplainingly, in the service of our family she had shut down her own career, and to this, as to so many other things, I'd been indifferent. The dailiness of cohabitation is like a rain of glass beads that wears away the larger perceptions of gratefulness and leaves behind only the chilly relicts of feeling. How could I have been so blind to the truth?

On the heels of this insight, I came to a decision. The decision, in so many words, was that I would act.

Once a month, Lucy spent the evening with her reading group, invariably returning from these evenings amiable and refreshed. Since that night was coming up, I chose it as the one on which to put my plan into action. I knew she'd be coming home that particular evening at seven, and instead of doing the usual thing (going out for Chinese with the boys, and bringing her back leftovers), I took off from work early, cut the boys' after-school playdates short, fed them sandwiches and palmed them off on an amiable elderly widower who lived nearby and owned a vast collection of antique pinball machines. Then I cleaned the house myself. Afterward, I shopped and made dinner. These small routine actions of preparation were rehearsals of a sort, isometric exercises designed to keep my good spirits pumped. I was ready, waiting and in a great mood when I heard the lip of her Subaru crunch on the front driveway.

"Well, hello, darling," I said as she came in the front door.

She had her battle face on; the eyes slitted, the mouth in a judging downward turn. Her eyes fell to the spatula in my hand. They rose to my apron and whisked quickly around the house. Then, nearly under her breath, she muttered, "You cleaned."

"Yup."

"And you . . . what . . ." She wrinkled her nose.

"Cooked? Yes, I did," I said quickly, "chicken simmered with wine and portobello mushrooms, and a bottle of your favorite Chianti to go with."

"I see," she said, slinging her bag to the floor. "And why?"

"Why? Because I wanted to celebrate."

"Celebrate?" She looked perplexed. "Celebrate what?"

"Us, for starters."

Her perplexity deepened. I knew the modulations of her face so well I could see small muscles in her cheeks, rarely used, coming in to play.

"Us?" she asked.

"The one and only." I made an embellishing motion with the spatula in the air.

She studied me for a moment. "Well, don't you seem jolly," she said. "Been into the cooking wine?"

"Come on."

"Where are the kids?"

"They're at Ferdie Pacheco's house."

Lucy commenced a small, somewhat tiptoed circuit of the kitchen, as if to assure herself that all was as tidy as it seemed. "That's impressive," she said, but in the same dead tone as previously. Then she turned and looked me full in the face for what felt like the first time in days. Inopportunely perhaps, but deeply, I was struck again by the wholesome symmetry of her features. Marathon stalemates have the advantage of absenting you long enough from your habitual tracks that when you return you can be surprised, as I was, by overlooked local pleasures. Lucy was beautiful.

"And all this is what," she asked, "reparations of a sort?"

"Hey, it worked for the slaves, didn't it?" I laughed in the silence, and spread my arms. When she didn't say anything more, I lowered them and leaned forward. "Look, I admit I've made mistakes, taken some things for granted, okay? Probably little parts of me fell asleep over the years, and I feel bad about that. I want you to know," I went on, "that I recognize how hard you work, and I want to honor it somehow." I heard the slightly canned quality to my speech, and said more softly, "Remember how I used to cook for you, honey?"

She shook her head to herself, sadly, a dreamy half smile on her face.

"I've been seeing a therapist," she said.

I felt a pang, deep in my stomach.

"Purefoy?"

"Yes."

I loathed the bald, handsome, self-impressed Purefoy. We'd first seen him not long after Will was born, when we'd grown frightened by the high wave of incomprehension and dead-calm indifference that seemed to be hurtling toward us. Still holding my arms up, I slowly lowered them to my sides.

"Well," I said, struggling to keep things light against a sudden sharp feeling of undertow, "I'm glad you've been talking to someone, because you certainly haven't been talking to me!" In the ongoing silence, I went on, "Hey, I've got an idea. How about let's have some of that wine you just accused me of drinking?"

"Fine."

I poured the Chianti, and nodding her thanks, she took a sip, set it down.

"Nick?"

"Yes, honey?"

Her large made-up eyes, ringed with mascara, stared deeply into mine. "Why are you trying to end this marriage?"

"What?" I cried.

"It's obvious, isn't it?" she said.

"No, it's not!"

"Oh, but it is," she said. "The doctor and I are in perfect agreement on this. And all the signs point to it."

"What signs are those?"

"I guess you know," she ignored my question, "that Deirdre Friedrich saw you and Belinda Castor at Padi-Cakes?"

My heart began thudding against my ribs.

"Well, how nice for Deirdre Friedrich," I said.

"She said that you two were laughing and carrying on like a house on fire. She used that very phrase, 'house on fire.'"

"So?" I said, ignoring the persistent banging at my clavicle, "Is that a crime? I mean, come on, honey. I took her out for a cup of tea. It seemed the least I could do under the circumstances. We talked mainly about Rob, her career, and the pain she was in. The woman is kind of inconsolable right now. And yes, all right, I did my best to make her laugh—so shoot me!"

In the extended silence, my smile drying on my face, both of us then listened to the distinct sound of me swallowing hard. When her voice next came it was gentler than I'd heard it in a long time.

"Do you think I don't know you, Nick? Do you really

believe you're living in some little tree house of the mind, spying out on the world and the world can't see you back?"

"What are you saying?"

"Please don't pretend to be thick. I hate when you do that. For the last half year I've tried to find you, in that faraway place you've been living. Not only for the boys, but, you know . . ." I saw her lip trembling; I knew how much this was costing her, and I wanted suddenly to protect her—but against what? Myself? "For us. I love so much about you, Nick, that I think it's going to kill me to say this, but I have to." She took a deep breath, drew herself erect. "Why don't you just admit you want out, and we can go from there?"

"Out?" I said. "What do you mean, Lucy, 'out'?"

"I mean that maybe if you had more time to spend in that past you're always mooning over, you'd be happier. And if you were happier, I'd be happier too, even if . . . we'd come to the end of something."

"This is crazy!" I said loudly.

But she only gave me the sad dreamy smile again. "Is it? According to Dr. Purefoy, the inability to let go of the past is a classic diagnostic trait of depression. But you're not even depressed, Nick. You're just selfish. You're literally too selfish to grow up. I think I've had enough of it."

A stroke of something like sleep went through me, a hot, cardiac sensation of fatigue that caused me to sag against the counter.

"Please," she said, and having discharged her weapon, she seemed visibly relieved, "can I have another glass of wine?"

Reaching robotically toward the bottle, I poured.

"You've made your position clear over these last few months since Rob Castor's death," she said. "Now I'm going to tell you *my* position. I've decided that I'm not going to stand in your way. If you want to leave this relationship, I will not oppose you."

"You will not oppose me," I repeated dully.

"Not even a little. There's no use in your staying around in a situation you so obviously want out of."

"Uh-huh," I said.

"My parents have said they'd help out if necessary, and I can always go back to work. Of course," she added, lowering her eyes as if in the grip of sudden modesty, "I remain open to any suggestions you might have to improve the situation."

I realized I was now clenching my jaw, a kind of strap-like torque running up the sides of my head.

"However"—she raised her eyes—"you'll have to be the one to initiate, Nick. It's humiliating to have to run after you like a personal assistant just to get a live response out of you. I know that 'communication' is not what you're especially good at. And I appreciate what you did tonight in cleaning the house and cooking. I appreciate what it might have to say about you showing up generally. Thank you. But a few good gestures do not a new life make."

The breezy tone of this last phrase, imported to show that she was detached from it all, made me feel worse. I loved her. Now, in fact, more than ever. Couldn't she see that? Didn't that mean something? Not knowing what else to do, I turned away, toward the stove.

"There is one place you *could* start, that is if you're interested," I heard her say.

"What's that?"

"I think you know."

"A vacation?"

"No."

I turned back around to face her. "Lemme guess. Purefoy."

"That's right."

"Dear God."

Had it been a dozen times that we'd gone there, a small, cowed couple, grateful for the crumbs thrown from his Olympian height? I couldn't remember how many visits we'd made, but I distinctly recalled the hissing wave sounds of his white-noise generator; I remembered the long silences in the oak-paneled office, the tactfully placed box of tissues, and the air of pretend normalcy beneath which, it was implied, abysses of nighttime dysfunction might be opened up to the healing, vitamin-packed light of day. Despite his studied neutrality, it had been my impression that the doctor disapproved of me in some way that surprised even himself. I did not want to see Dr. Purefoy.

"I'll think about it," I said.

"Your call."

I returned to preparing dinner, feeling as if tackled by a new gravity of sadness, and was just plating the food when Ferdie Pacheco returned early with the kids in his loud pickup truck. They piled into the house, and Lucy rushed to see them, and their obvious happiness in each other, something I'd approved of wholeheartedly and enabled as a foundational fact of our marriage, made me feel utterly wretched tonight. The emotional lockdown between us might have softened a bit as a result of our recent conversation; some warmth might have crept back in; but it was accompanied by a grim climate of finality anchored to an ultimatum. The boys were eager to show her some bauble that Pacheco had given them, and she followed them upstairs to their rooms without even a glance in my direction. I sat for a long while in front of the ebbing heat of my dinner, trying to digest what had just happened while listening to the familiar whooping hilarities proceeding from above.

# ....chapter 13 ...

I LEFT FOR MANHATTAN EARLY THE NEXT day. It was a Saturday, and I had no other pressing plans— save the one of getting some distance from my own family. About twice a year I drove down to New York, each time returning reliably refreshed from having hitched a ride on the sights and sounds of the speeding city. On impulse, I had called Mac the night before, while Lucy and the kids were still cavorting upstairs—she'd eventually returned to dinner, apologetic for having left the way she did—and had asked if he was available to pass a few hours. He'd said yes immediately, and then after a pause, asked if I'd heard the "big news." He'd received what he called "a juicy contract" to write the "definitive" book on Rob. As a result, he'd managed to rent, for a month, Rob's "horrendous" Chinatown apartment, which would help him "enter the mind of the madman." His voice was high and thin with excitement as he told me his news. Would I like to see him at Rob's place?

Standing in the house still in my absurd apron, feeling tender and sore, I hesitated a moment, wondering if I was up for it. Then I told him yes, I would, and I congratulated him a little rotely on his good fortune. I'd never trusted Mac completely, neither as a child nor as an adult. Up until high school he hadn't been nearly as close to Rob as I had. Later in life, he would be bound to Rob by style and affect and by the fact of writing too, but back in the early years of our lives, when the deepest chords were struck, he was just another roly-poly kid with a bad haircut and grass-stained pants. I had the inside track. I knew the secret tender things about Rob that no one else did. And I always would. Why, then, was it Mac grabbing the glory?

It was still dawn when I left the house. After three hours heading south in the blank box of the interstate, I entered New York by the Saw Mill River Parkway, twisting my way through the woods above Manhattan, and then driving down the West Side Highway. That first view of the city always struck me as something grand, nearly patriotic, with the big silver ripple of river alive with moving boats, the low-slung frame of Jersey on the right, and the heavy, leaden mass of buildings rising on the left and filled with cells of gloomy promise.

What was my promise? I was a man in a teetering marriage and a dead-end job whose future seemed to stretch before him in a succession of endless repetitions. As I threaded the big car through a series of narrowing highways, I consoled myself for these gloomy thoughts with unflattering recollections of the way Mac's professional personality had formed over the years, the lumps in it slowly smoothed out over repeated cycles of adaptation. At first, when he began writing for national magazines as a celebrity profiler, he made a point of being very haughty to us, his old school chums. He did this while still sucking up to the people useful to him, and this unstable balancing act between servility and pissiness seemed to prefigure the evolution of a truly awful person. He'd taken an apartment in downtown Manhattan somewhere, and on the rare occasions he came back to Monarch he made a point of either showily ignoring us, or, in a way I've since learned famous people do, being so over the top and effusive in his greeting that its obvious falsity is a different but equally offensive slap in your face.

By the time we were hitting our early thirties, success and having kids had softened him somewhat. Over the last year or so, his mom had been ailing, he was often in Monarch, and he'd opened himself up to us, his townies, by being the bearer of news about Rob. Since Rob's death, he'd been even more candid and thoughtful—with me in particular—than ever before. Yet somehow this didn't make me trust him. I knew that Mac had his own problems in life. I'd heard from other people that he'd developed a certain bitterness about the way in which, no matter how successful he was, it was still expected of him that he spend his days as a journalist applying rouge to the reputations of the rich and famous. He could be the dinner partner of real success, or be the roommate of success, or belong to the clubs where success sweated and worked out. He could watch success from up close and maybe even fuck it now and again, but he was never quite able to *be* it.

I turned off West Street, continued driving downtown.

Eventually I found myself threading streets that grew increasingly tight and crooked, like the sentences of some ancient document. Winding around Canal Street for a while, I parked finally in front of a small, shabby apartment house. The name of the street was Grand. I checked the address one last time and got out, rang the doorbell and was buzzed in.

Stepping into a dim entryway filled with the brackish smells of old cooking, I heard my name being called. I looked up through the boxed spiral of landings, and saw Mac's tiny face peering down at me from several floors above.

"Nicholas, my man!" he cried, his voice echoing down the stairwell.

"Mac, how are you?"

"Dandy. Come on up."

I began to climb the ancient sagging stairs. "Jesus, are you sure this will support my weight?" I asked.

"Well, you are a weighty kind of guy," cried Mac. When I got to the top, we shook hands. He was wearing jeans cut so as to emphasize his bulging thighs and he looked bigger up top since we'd last gotten together a few weeks earlier—weight lifting, most probably. His hair was waxed or gelled out into millipede spikes, and the skin on his cheeks had the rosy waxen cast of a man who's recently received professional spa attentions.

"I didn't know they let family men this far downtown." He slapped me on the back.

"Ha," I said. "Christ, did he actually live here?" We were walking down the hall. Moldy ferns of bubbled paint crawled up the walls; the grimed tiles underfoot were half missing; a strong urinous smell accompanied our progress. "I'm not sure that the word 'live' is correct," Mac said. "But this is where his body spent its last few weeks of life."

We entered the tiny cavelike apartment. Dozens of coats of white paint over the years had cocooned it in a kind of caked, sheltering softness. Off to one side, the kitchen was a mere nutritional indentation against a wall. A sink bore a big exploded brown stain in the center. I didn't want to look too closely. We completed the tour by entering the bedroom. The door was stuck closed on the repeatedly painted jamb. When it popped open, brilliant light flooded the whole apartment from the sunshine angling in over the Manhattan Bridge. It passed through a lattice of rusted window gates on its way. The place was a jail.

"You're paying to be here?" I asked.

"Field research," said Mac, with his half smile, "is a costly kind of thing. If nothing else"—we went back out and he opened the tiny ancient fridge, dark with beer bottles—"my advance will keep me in Strolsch for several years to come."

He retrieved two beers, and presented one to me with a frontal push of the beer into my hand. We clinked bottles.

"To our dear pal," I said.

"'Hid in death's dateless night,'" Mac intoned. "Have a seat, Nick."

At the kitchen were two mismatched ladder-back chairs. I sat in one, trying to smile at Mac, my mind whirling.

"You look upset," he said, staring at me keenly a second.

"Yeah, well, I guess I am. I mean, I knew he was down

on his luck toward the end, but Christ I had no idea that it was . . . like *this*. I might have been happier without knowing, actually."

"I hear you, pal. It was like he wanted to punish himself."

"Was it," I gestured vaguely, "just like this when you found it?"

"More or less. Chin, the scumbag landlord, took most of his stuff, I think, including his Grundig shortwave and his rose-quartz collection and who knows what else. But I did get the book." He nudged with his chin toward a Sears bag on the floor.

"The book?"

"The diary. Shirley got it actually, probably because it was just in a shitty loose-leaf binder, and Chin overlooked it. I bought it from her. Wanna see it?"

"Yes," I said instantly, "I do."

He reached into the bag and withdrew a loose-leaf binder, thickly stuffed with what seemed hundreds of pages. On closer inspection it appeared to have been covered in bark of some sort, with holes bored through the covers, and twine twisted through these holes.

"What the hell is this?" I asked.

"Some shamanistic thing," said Mac, handing me the notebook and shaking his head. "Rob was so *Serpent and the Rainbow* sometimes it drove me nuts."

He went to the beer vault, opened it and got another. "I'm going to go take some notes on the view out the bedroom window." He saw me looking at the diary. "Go ahead, read it"—he turned away—"it won't bite. At least," he added with a laugh, "it hasn't yet."

With a certain trepidation I opened the rough covers. In block letters were the words "My Final Resting Place," with some shakily drawn flowers below them. On the next page I saw the familiar script, but more sloppy and urgent than I remembered. I looked quickly around the room, as if to alert the ghost of Rob to what I was about to do, and then dropped my eyes.

*Bang!* I read. *So you're finally here, friend. I've been waiting for you my whole life long, and now you've arrived. My ideal reader! For all the thousands of long hours leading up to this moment, have you any idea of how immensely comforting has been the thought of you? Can I add that I've wondered long about what you'd look like, what you're bringing to this act this very minute, the color of your eyes, your hair, the way these words feel, moving through your nerves?*

*I'd like to apologize up front for the state of things and the mess I'll leave behind. I would have liked a tight surgical suture at the end of my life——a six-gun salute, the sharp military report and six smoky volutes rolling above the Monarch village green. I was always attracted to the nakedness of the military world, its dyadic simplicities: yes, no, enemy or friendly, alive or dead.*

*Speaking of dead: if you're reading this, I'm already gone. But let's talk a little bit about you,* caro lettore. *Did you know that, while I was alive, every cruel thing you and your friends said about me killed me another inch? I used to sit among you in the bars of Manhattan, and I used to hear the silly, vain conversations leaving your mouths, and I would think to myself: but these aren't people speaking words, this is the sound of money itself,* speaking through the lips of people, the uproar of coins clanging against each other, and bills rubbed with a hiss to make a little warmth exit those lipsticked mouths, those strong athletic jaws. How excited you were to have arrived at your metropolitan eminence, and how convinced that the entire history of the planet to date was just a dim prelude to your own dazzling turn on the stage of life. You didn't realize that generation after generation of New Yorkers had sung the very same song of acquisition as you, moved just as you were by the immensities of used feeling that song contained. They'd roared themselves hoarse for the same teams as you; grown indignant over the same municipal cruelties and ecstatic over the same real estate. They'd had the same "breakthroughs" in psychotherapy as you and privately drawn the same perimeter lines around themselves to mark their own behavior off as more noble and anguishingly subtle than their friends'. Manhattan had seen it all before, my friend, and was laughing its head off at you.

But I didn't laugh. No, I loved you. I couldn't explain it even to myself, but my love for you was enormous. My love filled the streets and buildings and the hollow bellies of the city which are veined with subways and blown through with the miserable famished dust of the poor. I loved you, all of you, and yet somehow, increasingly, it was not enough.

It was not enough to have written my heart out in red streams of ink for you, exhausting myself in acts of witnessing. Not enough to have loved the romance of literature, its inner histories of mankind, and to have served it as faithfully as I knew how for many years; or to try to meet a woman fully, nakedly and deeply; or to be a good son, a brother and a friend.

It was not enough to ascend a summit of awareness and look around me while ignoring the signal-clotted preponderance of the material world which surrounds us, leans into us, drills us full of numbness and dead air, and then whips those moribund inner spaces into the desire to have and possess. I wanted to possess nothing. I was indifferent to the claims of ownership. There is a reason all religions, no matter their outlooks, converge in the understanding that the visible world is merely a beautiful shawl of energy which we briefly don before returning to its rightful owner. The greatest returns in life are symbolic. Man makes tools but he is a riser and a lifter. He raises crops and lifts his voice in song. And he believes.

When I was very young, and happily paranoid in that way of small, mother-loved children, I was briefly convinced that the entire planet was peopled with cunning robots perfectly resembling humans, and likewise certain that I was the last uncolonized member of my race. I grew out of that. Or at least thought I had. But in reality, I underwent a mere suspension of insight, a thirty-year hiatus of understanding. Because everywhere I look now I see the signs of membership in that same tribe of the electric dead. The inert, dreamlike shuffling of people in the New York streets. The stink of the dead, black and sulfurous, pouring out of the mouths of subway stations and the necropolises of skyscrapers. The marble inertia of the past lying heavy on all things.

No one knows how easy it is to be perfectly alone in the midst of that tumbling stillness. I'm living now in a state of keen pre-grief for what I'm about to do upon finishing this page. I'm going to leave this apartment and look directly into the dragon's mouth. It may involve violence, but if it does, so be it. The rest of this journal can serve as a charming little cautionary tale for those who believe they can warm their hands easily at the fire of "art," and play at being creative. The dangers are very real. Poetry is a blood jet. I washed my face in it but it would not come clean. Good-bye, dear reader. Your friendship was almost enough, but not quite. Not nearly. And the flood flowers now.

# PART THREE

# chapter 14

FOR A GOOD LONG WHILE, ACCORDING to Mrs. Halasz, the soft singsong voice of Rob continued in the apartment above her. Suddenly, she said, his voice grew loud, as if remonstrating or arguing a point. After this, abruptly, silence fell. Soon the silence was supplanted by yet another noise—running water.

Kate was taking a shower. She'd used the bathroom, and was taking a shower. All of us later admitted this was an extraordinary move. Grimed and deranged, Rob was sitting in the sunny kitchen, a .38 in his pocket and his heart in his mouth, and Kate was standing in the needling shower water, soaping her body.

In the words of a hostage negotiator who later testified at the trial, she was doing exactly what she should have been doing under the circumstances and "gaining trust." From the moment she'd gotten out of bed, the negotiator explained, she'd been signaling to Rob her complete indifference to the danger, and thereby establishing "a faith axis" along which the two of them might speak. By acting as if there was no danger at all, went this logic, she might possibly replicate that calm in the wider world.

She showered for about ten minutes. Then she apparently spent a while brushing her hair. After that, strangely, she put on makeup. This detail intrigued just about everybody: base, blusher, eye shadow, eyeliner, and to finish it all off, a couple of swipes of the oxblood matte brown lipstick she liked. Painted as if for a night out—even if she rarely wore makeup, no matter the occasion—she exited the bathroom, having swapped her towel for a fluffy white bathrobe, and sat down across from Rob, who was still sitting where she'd left him.

In the face of her newly groomed beauty, her calm, her apparent availability, he was almost certainly stunned. For a minute or two he might have felt himself returned to a previous moment in time, and to be again staring at the fresh, utterly poised small-town girl with whom he was going to take literary New York by storm. Perhaps as he relaxed back into that dream he was able as well to look around himself and see the rank absurdity of his recent life—the gun, the crazed pursuit, the death by inches of his days in the room in Chinatown. It's entirely possible that he returned wholly to himself for a brief moment and told himself that everything, incredibly, might just work out fine.

Mrs. Halasz testified that a sudden and complete silence ensued, abruptly followed by the squealing of chairs on the floor. The silence lasted several minutes, and was followed by the beginning of a new kind of sound, one which, according to Mrs. Halasz, sent her scurrying out of the kitchen and into the bedroom to stop her ears.

They were having sex. Loudly, passionately, in their old apartment, they were having sex. "Like wolves," Mrs. Halasz told the court, her lip curling disgustedly. Cries and shouts, she said, pursued her around the apartment as she fled from room to room, and they seemed to go on for hours.

When it was over, a postcoital lull followed. In those tangled spearmint sheets, in that moment of midmorning when New York City comes alive with a sudden rush of fury—whatever did they talk about then? Having rehearsed an act of love, even one coerced, did they pretend that the intervening months were simply a folly, a tragic parenthesis of sorts? Did Rob, always one to exalt his own feelings, speak candidly to her of what it was like to experience his mind unhitching itself from its moorings and drifting out to sea? If that were the case, then doubtless Kate listened closely, and maybe, animated by some passing whiff of charity, she gave in to the human impulse to help this person whom she had just permitted into her body, and with whom she'd once shared a dream. Perhaps she held him, calmed his fears, drew his head to her breast and stroked his hair, while talking to him about mythic love, and improbable passion under extreme circumstances. Perhaps, with brilliantly tactical tenderness, she wiped his brow and recalled him to an earlier day. And then the phone rang. Her answering machine was turned up to 10 and the phone was ringing. When the answering machine picked up, the voice began to speak.

At the trial, visibly on the edge of tears, Framkin now

took the stand. Pale and drawn, he'd lost the prosperous belly of once upon a time. After the murder, the tabloid press had feasted on him without letup and picked the bones of his reputation clean in a frenzy. Looking out at the courtroom with the ashen majesty of a deposed monarch, he said that yes, he'd placed that call, and had done so from the Taconic State Parkway—a detail he was sure of because he remembered that he'd been staring out the window at the hillsides of perfectly ranked passing trees and was struck by how that orderly processional somehow reminded him of Kate. He remembered as well the strong morning sun shining as he picked up the phone and, speaking calmly and affectionately, signed his lover's death warrant.

"Darling girl" read his phone message, transcribed and printed up in seventy-two-point type and displayed on large easels at the trial, "I'm missing you so much right now that it's driving me half mad. Where are you, baby? Do you want some of that bedside manner? Do you want me to come over right now and make everything all right in that special way? God, do I want you. I've still got your smell on me. Call when you can. 'Bye, sweet girl."

Hundreds, perhaps thousands, of times, he said, he'd imagined what had happened as those words of his floated out upon the still air of that sunny room. What did happen, exactly, we will never know. What we do know is that five minutes later, with Kate lying calmly in her bed, a shot rang out, reverberating with terrifying volume in the spaces of the old building. Mrs. Halasz rushed out her door, but when she got into the grimy stairwell, with its gray marine light entering through pebbled old windows, and its floor of buckled dull tile like a heaving sea, her heart began to beat heavily in her chest, and overcome with fear, she ran back into her apartment, locked all three locks and dialed 911.

Rob meanwhile walked out of the building and into the living world. Over the next few hours his movements were simple, schematic and easily traced. He shoved a bloodstained shirt into a nearby Dumpster—later recovered. He went to the Port Authority and caught a bus for Monarch—paying for it with a credit card. And that night, at New Russian Hall, he showed up unannounced and shocked us all.

As it turned out, there were only a few of us there when the door opened and Rob walked in. I, for one, did my best to hide my astonishment. As an adult, unless he was drunk, Rob had never liked large emotions and outsize public demonstrations, and so I welcomed him back with deliberately low-key surprise, gave him a subdued high five and drew him to the bar. I noticed that his long blond hair hung lusterless; that the bones of his face had become prominent. I noticed that his hand trembled, slightly, as he reached for his stein.

But mainly I was deeply happy to see him—especially because it had been so long since any of us had glimpsed him without a girlfriend in tow or a meeting to which he had to speed.

Word of his presence spread quickly by cell phone. Within a half hour, a full barroom quorum would be reached, and the evening would blend into that typically whirling muddle of alcohol, geysers of animation and sodden wit that was the conclusion of nearly every Friday night out. But before Mac arrived, and the others with him, there was still time to ask Rob how he was doing, and watch a small faraway smile come over his face, and the ring on his pinkie finger begin clicking against the glass of his beer, and him look up with all the patient sadness in the world and say softly, "Terrible, man, just terrible." There was still time, before the crowds poured in, when it was easy to notice that a strange resignation hung about him like a mist, and that he looked at all of us with a faintly marveling expression, as if he were already halfway to the next world and glancing back over his shoulder to see us laboring still in fields of irrelevant human sleep.

"Nick," he said softly, at one moment, as the cars began pulling up outside, their lights spearing through the windows, "Nick, God, it's been a strange ride."

"Has it, Rob?" I asked.

He looked at me a second. "You're a gentle guy," he said, "and you always were. Don't lose that, you know?"

"I-I won't," I said, suddenly feeling frightened.

"Because you won't know when it goes," he said as car doors slammed outside. "It leaves no sign that it's gone, that kindness, but once it does, it never comes back. Never ever. That's the mistake most people make—they think it's learned. The hell it is." He lit a cigarette, and I saw how skinny his wrists and fingers had become; the nails were individually nibbled to the quick, the cuticles frayed. "It's just an endowment, like blue eyes or curly hair, but with one difference. It gets used up. And what replaces it"—he looked around the bar with an eerie, haunted look coming over him that made me cold in the pit of my stomach—"ain't nice."

He was still shaking his head gently at me as the advance team of old friends crashed through the front door and let out a long, warlike whoop of joy.

Rob moved very little that night. He sat at the bar and received people and seemed to accept the affection extended to him without surprise. After our brief exchange, I hung near, laughing along with the jokes and raising my beer in the endless toasts, while wondering, with a small inner part of myself, what it would have been like to have been loved like that in life; to be desired and admired as an outstanding example of something. I couldn't help but feel, looking at him without knowing I was witnessing the beginning of the end of his life, that he was a genius after all for having chosen a path that had brought such power to him, and such light and such acclaim.

The evening tilted, deepened, grew louder. Waves of admirers seemed to wash up to him, recede back into the bar, drinks in hand, and then surge forward again. And amid those social tides, he sat as fixed as a rock, nodding, smiling occasionally, but mostly saying nothing, already gone.

Certainly in the course of that evening he was asked about Kate. Almost certainly he responded in some way or another that managed to deflect the thrust of the question. But none of us remembers. Strangely enough, there seems a dearth of detailed memory among all of us as regards that night, a kind of extended blank or leached-out spot, like a videotape passed too close to a strong magnet. What we can recall is that while he was sad and abstracted, very thin and very subdued, he bore no fatal disfiguring marks of the assassin. No fateful portents. There was nothing in him for example to indicate that a dozen or so hours earlier, crouching over the supine form of his ex-beloved, he'd carefully shot her right between her green eyes.

# chapter 15

THE LETTER ARRIVED WHILE I WAS AT work, filling out grant applications. It was short, direct and typed on a piece of cheap notepaper. *"We need to talk,"* it read.

> *The Zen masters have a term for what they believed to be predestined togetherness. It is "Innen." My mind has been racing since seeing you. It's like this roaring sound in my head. But it ain't the surf, buddy boy. I don't wanna scatter the twigs of your little marital nest, but I simply have to see you again.*
>
> *Of course, that's just my point of view. You may have an entirely different one. If the phone rings at 310-999-3434 over the next week, and if it's you on the other end, then I'll know that my point of view was right after all.*
>
> *B.*

Quickly, without thinking about it, nudging the office door shut with a foot before I could come to my senses, I dialed the number.

A moment later her low voice said, "Nicky."

"Hi, Belinda. You knew it was me?"

I thought I heard the rasp and hiss of a cigarette being lit. "Yeah, you're at work, right?"

"Yes I am."

"Poor you. How's it going?"

"The usual, pretty boring. I wish I were somewhere else."

"Mmm. I wish you were somewhere else too," she said. "Do you?"

"Yes."

"That's mighty neighborly of you," I said, and laughed. There was a pause.

"I want you, Nick," she said.

At that, the room went away; the buzzing fluorescent lights, the slab wooden desk, the framed Western prints and worn coatrack—all of it gone. From a distance, with the slightly dazed affect of one who has just, with perfect timing, detonated a stick of dynamite in his own face, I heard myself say slowly, "And me you."

"I thought I wouldn't, but hey, I do," she said.

"It's as if ever since seeing you," I said, "even when I wasn't thinking about you, I was."

"There's this way"—her voice was sinking, soft—"that life has of pushing certain people into your life so often and so freaking brilliantly that you finally say, okay, I get it. Do you understand what I'm saying?"

"I think so."

"Do you?"

"Un-huh."

"Can we talk about your mouth?"

I felt a kick in my lower abdomen.

"Belinda," I said.

"Can we talk about lust, that crazy human experience?"

"Sweetie."

"Can we talk about my desire to suck your cock, Nick?"

I braced a hand on my brow, and shut my eyes.

"You look good, Nick. I want that goodness. I want to ride that kiss in the car to some old and happy place. Don't tell me that's selfish."

Unbidden, a wave of sexual images flooded my brain. "It's a little difficult right now," I said haltingly, "at home, you know."

"What, in the perfect marriage?" she snorted. "In that little Potemkin village you call home? Don't tell me that rain is falling in Disneyland. That'd be too sad for words."

"Please don't attack my home life," I said. "As it happens, we're in a kind of delicate place."

"Are you."

"Kind of."

"I thought you'd never been so happy."

"Did I say that?"

"That very phrase, Nick."

I was silent. After a moment, she went on, "I don't mean to barge in on you in a bad moment, honey. I was surprised by how great it was to see you. But I'll go away if you want me to. Is that what you want?"

A long, fraught sigh emptied itself out of my chest. Was that what I wanted? Lucy was everything I'd ever

desired in a woman, save one thing. And Belinda was nothing but that thing. Did I want her to go away? She was Rob
Castor's sister, after all, and all that was really left of him
in the world. The two even shared the same physical traits:
the sidling swagger, the proud nose and the deep-set blue
eyes.

"No," I said, "it's not what I want."

"Oh, frabjous day," she said. "Well, that's a fucking
relief."

There was a pause.

"Hey, Belinda?"

"Yeah?"

"I have to ask you something."

"Shoot."

"Are you stoned?"

She made an astonished sound. "Why would you say
such a thing, Nick? And the answer is yes, of course I am.
But when did that ever make a difference?"

"No," I said, "I was just wondering if that was the
reason for this phone call, is all."

"Oh, please. You called me, remember?"

"True," I said, "but you sent me—" I stopped myself.

"Thank you," she said, "for not being quite that small.
And by the way, please don't do the disapproving family-
man thing with me—I can't stand that shit."

"Sorry."

"Or is your self-esteem so low you think I'd have to be
wasted to be attracted to a guy as white as you?"

We both laughed.

"Good old Belinda."

"Listen," she said happily, "the deal is this. I'm heading

back to Monarch in a few weeks, and I'll be there for a month or so, staying at a hotel in town. Yeah," she snorted, "Hiram and I are going to stage an intervention on my mom. Isn't that a scream?"

"It's sad is what it is," I said. "Poor old thing."

"Pity," she said, "is a luxury I can't afford. I'll call you when I get in, all right?"

"Great."

"'Bye, darl." And then, with a strange adhesive sound that I realized only later was a drunken kiss, Belinda hung up the phone.

# chapter 16

DR. PUREFOY SAT PERFECTLY POISED AND erect in front of us. He swept his coolly compassionate gaze around the air over our heads. Sporting a deep winter tan, he was wearing a brown cashmere suit and low-slung bifocal glasses.

"Go on," he said.

"The thing is"—Lucy looked at him, blinking with intensity—"he *has* begun making efforts. But it doesn't cure the larger problem, which is that in a fundamental way, he's simply not there and hasn't been for a while."

The doctor gave a quick compassion-flex of the underside of his mouth, and nodded.

"Not there," he repeated gravely.

In the half hour or so we'd already been there, Lucy had monopolized the conversation in a fluent diagnostic aria about the state of our marriage. Her color was high, her posture was erect, and I'd soon realized that she was *enjoying* it; that it was *fun* for her.

"I thought that in a way we had both made our peace with our respective roles in the marriage. We'd buried a lot of our differences for the sake of the children. Maybe we even had an unspoken contract to let the spool run out until the kids left home and then take stock. Is that," she asked, a bit plaintively, "really so unusual?"

But Dr. Purefoy was not about to be drawn into a direct response.

"Go on," he said.

"But then what happened is, a few months ago, right around the time of Rob Castor's death, Nick seemed to enter a new phase of being distracted. I was used to it up to a point, but not *this*. It wasn't even gradual, Doctor. It was like the husband I'd known was body-snatched one night while I slept. In a very real way, things haven't been the same since."

I knew that Lucy had been seeing Purefoy alone for several weeks, and sitting there, I had the highly unpleasant sense that this conversation was something prearranged between the two of them in a subtle way, and that I had, in so many words, walked into a trap. Holding the doctor's measuring gaze, I said, "Excuse me, but how common is it for a therapist such as yourself to begin with a single person and then, after having worked with that person awhile, begin seeing that person's spouse in couples therapy?"

"You're questioning my methods," said Purefoy amiably, looking at me.

"No, I'm just asking."

"There is no 'just' about it, Nick," the doctor replied, his cheerful expression falling with a rapidity that was, it occurred to me, a therapeutic technique of some sort. "You are posing a challenge to my authority to be here. Is there something in this situation you find uncomfortable? Are you perhaps threatened by the candor of this discussion?"

Quietly, unobtrusively over the previous half hour, I'd been studying Dr. Purefoy. The fake gravities of the face; the stylized sympathetic shrugs of the shoulders; the way he shook his head heavily from side to side to indicate the depths, the chambered profundities of his heart—I thought Purefoy was a hack. I thought he was a bad actor playing a role. In his mind, no doubt, my hostility toward him was the simple side effect of how much I had to hide. But for the most part, sitting there for a half hour had reinforced the opinion I'd formed from my experience with him ten years earlier: I didn't like the man.

"I'm not threatened," I said calmly, and noticed out of the side of my eye that Lucy was staring down at her shoes, "and furthermore, if you'll pardon me, I think that my question was a reasonable one."

Purefoy gave a rare full smile and steepled his hands together in an attitude of superior indulgence.

"Nick," he said, "the process we're embarked upon together today is composed of many layers. To get to those deeper layers requires a certain transparency between us to function effectively. Certainly, as you know, I've had several sessions already with your wife, and during those sessions we've endeavored, among many other things, to reconstruct what it is you're attempting to signal through your actions of late. But my relationship with you falls under the exact same therapeutic purview as mine with hers, no more, no less. I'd be happy to see you separately if you prefer, but it is my sincere belief that there is much to be gained from cutting through those layers together, cutting, as it were," said the doctor suavely, "while collectively holding the knife."

His smile deepened. It was impossible not to notice how attractive the doctor believed himself to be; impossible not to notice how *installed* he felt in this room.

"Okay," I said.

"Very good."

There was a long silence during which, to my dismay, I felt a growing need to propitiate the man, break the silence. I said finally, "I do agree with Lucy that I'm trying more, to show up in the relationship and in life generally, and be more 'present,' to use that word"——I smiled at Lucy, who looked away——"my wife seems to love."

Head nod, lip flex, and a new moue consisting of the entire skull rotated into a forty-five-degree slant. I had to give him this: the doctor was expressive with minimal means. On top of that, he made me persistently uncomfortable, which was probably a kind of achievement.

"At the same time," I went on, "I'm aware that I have a way of absenting myself, and in my relationship with Lucy, I suppose that there was a way in which I simply locked myself away in my head, and didn't come out, for years."

"I see."

"But then again, I had a lot to deal with. You saw us

back then, so you know how green we were when it came to raising kids, running a home, et cetera."

"Yes," the doctor allowed.

"My feeling is that we got better at it, and that things threw us less, as time went on. But then Rob Castor died and I got all shook up by that, and Lucy claims that I've been different ever since. I don't know."

"Ah," the doctor said delicately. Again the long hands were steepled together. "And why would the death of Rob Castor have affected you so?"

"We were best friends when I was a kid, and I lost my brother when I was still pretty young, and Rob kind of stepped into that role. I suppose in an unconscious way I've always defined myself against him."

It felt good, in a general way, to be talking out loud, airing my concerns and off-loading some of the weight of built-up feeling in my chest. I was in the midst of the first self-congratulatory moment of the session when I heard Lucy's voice, low, saying, "And the sister."

"The sister?" the doctor asked as I felt my hands involuntarily tighten on the armrests of the chair.

"Belinda," she said. "A kind of failed rock-and-roll singer who has been sniffing around Nick ever since Rob died."

"Is this true?" Purefoy again turned his gaze on me.

"Is what true?"

"That there has been contact between you and this person?"

A hot flare of hatred passed through my chest. I said mildly, "I did go have a cup of tea with Belinda Castor a few weeks ago, yes. She's an old girlfriend, and I'd missed her at Rob's memorial service, because she was too messed up to come. We have a special kind of understanding because we're maybe the two people in the world who knew Rob best, and that means something."

There was a long silence.

"I think Nick has been talking to her at work," Lucy said, blindsiding me.

The doctor nodded his head as if expecting this, and pointed his chin like a bayonet at my chest. I crossed my arms.

"That's ridiculous!" I laughed.

"Is it?" he asked.

"Of course it is!" I was trying for an indignant tone but my voice came out thin and unconvincing.

The silence that followed went on for so long that the inadvertent noises of the sitting room came forward: a hissing of the heating unit, the smothered honk of a car horn in the street. When the doctor spoke, it was softly.

"I think we're ready to conclude for now," he said, "and I'd like to thank both of you for the brave, important work you've done today."

I couldn't understand how the "work" we'd just done was either brave or important, but now Purefoy was standing up, as were we, and he was shaking my hand with a straight-from-the-shoulder masculine grip of crushing force. The eyes, teeth and skull of the doctor were gleaming like a single enormous many-faceted head-light. Dazed, I let my arm drop and was mumbling thanks when Lucy stepped in front of him and turned upward to glance at him. Perhaps she also rose toward him from within her shoes. It was just a quick and passing glance, but it shook me for the deep understanding it bespoke. I'd be talking to her in the future about that glance, I thought.

Quietly, heads down, we left his office.

# chapter 17

UNBEKNOWNST TO ME, MY PARENTS NEVER quite stopped thinking about my brother. His presence, for them, continued to inhere in all sorts of anguishing little ways around the house. I didn't realize that their lives were forever tied to the remembered weights and measures of his body as it sat in chairs, thumped up and down stairs, or crossed hallways, running. I didn't understand that their hearts were stabbed on a daily basis by the clear recollections of his face and voice coming toward them through the air above the kitchen table and backyard. It was all, finally, too much for them to bear. Which is why, in my senior year in college, my dully predictable parents did something that shocked me to the core: they moved away.

Taking advantage of a surprise buyout of my father's small chemical company by American Pharmaceutical, they committed the entirely untypical act of retiring at the age of fifty-five and leaving Monarch for a seniors' community in Arizona with the radiantly dull name of Sunnyside Acres. A huge hecatomb of tin-roofed bungalows called "villas," Sunnyside Acres is a little pretend spa of sorts, with its own gym, its own theater, and its own artificial lake, containing a variety of torpid trout and at least nine disoriented swans. Days there are heavily scripted, as jammed with activities as that brother community in retirement, the cruise ship, and for similar reasons: the better to allow residents to ignore the grim, statistical ticking of the clock.

My parents have been there about a dozen years, and in the process this anxious shut-down couple have somehow reinvented themselves as precociously jazzy seniors. My father has taken up golf, a pastel wardrobe and the habit of midday cocktails. He's begun experimenting with a newly extroverted personality that is full of peppy bad jokes and pretend elder-statesman observations. My mother meanwhile has become a bird-watcher, as well as an avid member of the book club and the Mozart group. As for me, my relationship with them has never quite recovered from the shock of their sudden removal. On our once-a-month phone calls my mother still clucks affectionately and worries about me as one would a son seemingly adrift in his phase of "finding himself." And my father, from the vantage of his new personality, treats me like a slightly slow, humorless person with whom he once, many years ago, shared a particularly long vacation.

I called them the day after our session with Purefoy. I was certain that the actorly therapist with his canned responses had had no impact at all on me. But evidently being trapped in the cross fire of my wife and Purefoy together had affected me more than I knew. That night I'd been quite agitated, finding it difficult to sleep, erotic hankerings mixed with the sudden desire to weep, anger at Lucy alternating with scenarios in which, on bended knee, I begged for forgiveness. Out of this mess of feelings, a long-buried container of memory surfaced. And once prised open, the volatile contents of that container continued to spill without stopping.

When I reached my father, he was returning from a round of golf. He had his happy voice on, and I was certain he'd drunk a "Tanqueray with a twist" in the club-house before returning home. I could see him sitting down on the couch in his sky-blue shorts and his sport cap, his face drawn back into its genial old-guy lines, the phone at his ear.

"Hello, sonny boy, how's life?" he asked. When he's happy he calls me sonny boy.

"Fine, Dad. How're you doing these days?"

"Fit as a fiddle and pretty as a peach," he said, then he sighed in a way I'd never heard him sigh before and smacked his lips. The combination of sounds seemed to indicate a world of sizzling appetite, and I suddenly wondered about the precise nature of my father's friendship with any of the handsome, heavily rouged widows I'd seen greeting him effusively on the flagstone walking paths.

"Dad, I've been thinking."

"Stop the presses, my son has been thinking!"

"Right. Well anyway, I don't know why, but I've been in this phase of kind of being reflective about things, and I had this memory surface during the night."

"Did you now."

"I did, and it kinda ate at me."

"Don't you hate when that happens?"

"What, Dad?"

I thought I heard ice cubes clinking. It became clear to me that he was moving around the room.

"When you remember the bad stuff? I mean, what's the point? Live for today, the Good Book says. Am I right?"

"Right. Well, anyway, Dad, I was thinking about this time at the beach."

"Un-huh, yes."

"It must have been, oh, twenty-five or so years ago, maybe even thirty."

"Did I know you then? Had we been introduced?"

"Funny, Dad."

"I do my best."

"We were at Sandy Hook, with Mom and Patrick."

Definitely, I was certain, he was making a gin and tonic. I heard the plop of cubes and the gurgle of liquid being poured.

"You drinking?" I asked.

"Some, but not enough."

"I thought the doctor told you you had to stop."

"He did say I had to stop, he just didn't say when."

A self-delighted chuckle, followed by another sigh, this one, clearly, an accompaniment to sitting down in a chair or on the couch, chilled drink in hand, prepared for a trip down memory lane.

"I'm all yours," he said.

And so I told him. I told him about that moment in time when he'd been stretched out on a lounge chair one sunny afternoon many years ago during a rare family vacation at the beach, the surf crumpling a distance off, and my mom lying next to him, asleep in a one-piece suit with a frilly bit of skirt covering her thighs. I brought him back to remembering that skirt, and remembering the pushing heat of the day, and the open sound of the water. And I recalled him as well to how much effort he'd put into setting up our little camp, the trudging to and from the car through hot, floury sand to lug our basket of thermoses and sandwiches, and at the end of his effort, the prize of lying on the beach for a while, cooled by the stiff salt breeze and reading one of his beloved John D. MacDonald novels.

"God, I loved those trips," my father interrupted me, taking a long, swilling drink. The real pleasure in his voice surprised me. I'd always thought of him as living life in a kind of ongoing drab sufferance, but listening to him now, it suddenly occurred to me that it was perhaps only toward me he'd banked his fire, and that by this logic, incredibly, he might all along have been having a great time.

"And do you remember, Dad, that moment when I tried to show you my prize starfish in a bucket, and tripped and poured a torrent of cold water and sand into your lap?"

A beat of silence. And then in a slightly lower, more cautious voice: "I'm not sure I do, sonny boy."

"Really?" I pressed my case. "You were asleep at the time, I think. Don't you remember jumping to your feet in shock?"

The cubes clinked.

"Nope."

"Or how you leaned down to me, and this I'll never forget because I was such a little kid that it was like a tower, Dad, a tower darkening the sun. And you cursed at me? Do you remember what you said?"

"On the advice of my attorney Mr. Tanqueray"—he laughed at his own joke—"I can't remember a thing."

"You called me a bastard."

Silence. Even the sportive tinkle of the cubes had gone dead.

"Yeah, Dad, and the reason I remember it so well," I went on, "is because Mom jumped to her feet and she started screaming something at you, and she kind of drove you along the beach, like a smaller animal tormenting a bigger one, yeah, sort of like a mother bear attacking a male. The females are smaller, you know, but in defense of their own cubs they become kind of crazy and will do anything, even risk their own hide. Isn't that right? Dad?"

Again a long, deep, many-roomed sigh.

"Are we getting to the point on this one?" my father asked.

"Of course we are, Dad. I've just been thinking so much lately, about my own life and stuff, and the past especially. Maybe it's my"—I made quotation marks in the air with my voice—"'midlife crisis,' or who knows what, but I've been kind of looking at the way we all were as a family, Dad, and the life you had, all of you, with Patrick before I came along, and how much you loved him, you in particular. The funny thing is that, of course, I always thought it was just me, what I deserved from you, that incredible coldness you showed me, like there was something wrong I'd done to you just by being alive, you know."

"Dear God," my father said, his mouth partly away from the receiver, to the air.

"Don't get upset, Dad. I'm just explaining that as a kid, you take the way people treat you to be a kind of judgment on your own self, you've got no defenses, and so how you were to me, the indifference and so forth, it was like a condemnation of sorts, maybe it wasn't a death sentence, but boy was it close! And so I guess what I'm asking, and thanks again for your patience, Dad, is: did you mean 'bastard' as in a little piece of shit, or what, exactly? Dad?"

There was no sound at all. And for a moment, waiting, I held my breath. But then I realized that in some way I hadn't detected, very quietly and stealthily he had replaced the receiver. By the time the transistorized voice came on, asking me to hang up please, I was gently setting the phone back in the cradle—and then staring at it for several long seconds while resisting the sudden, furious temptation to smash it to bits.

# chapter 18

THE NEXT NIGHT, THE SNOW BEGAN FALL-
ing. It was the first snow of the season, and it fell with
perfect timing, for Christmas was approaching, and the
snowfall, for that, seemed a civic gesture entirely in keeping with the town fire department stringing lights, the
stores at the local strip mall bannering their windows with
big sale signs, and the festive feeling of an approaching
commercial apocalypse. I drove home from work, parked
outside in my driveway, and for a moment, rather than go
inside, I sat in the car while the aerial rivers of light, dry-
seeming snowflakes pattered against the windshield.

For reasons I wasn't entirely sure of, the conversation
with my father, as unsatisfying as it had been, had also
been directional: it had steered my mind inevitably toward
thoughts of my own sons.

Given the current situation at home, I hadn't been
nearly as attentive to Dwight and Will as I would have

liked over the past weeks or months, and I knew it. It ate at me to think that I might in some way be installing between us that same uphill grade I'd had to climb to meet my own father, growing up. At the same time, strangely and for the very first time, I had the nagging thought that my recent detachment was producing an opening or opportunity of a sort for someone else. I began believing that, as regarded my sons, this aloofness of mine, especially given how ambivalent Lucy seemed of late, might be encouraging—was it possible?—a potential rival.

I got out of the car and entered the house, determined somehow to right the situation. During dinner that night, spying on my family from behind the mask of my own affability, I studied all the subtle ways in which Lucy bound the children to her—ways, I told myself, that had nothing to do with the more obvious attachments of motherhood. It was the warm, nutritive comfort of her gaze as it swept over them, rounding them up into a collective overseen entirely by her. It was that way she projected a fitted love-utopia, unique to each of the boys. It stung me that they turned to her on reflex when they skinned a knee or barked a shin. It hurt that inevitably their jokes were hatched looking gleefully into her face for a first response. I asked myself if things had always been like this, or was I noticing it for the first time. Along with that question came the painful insight that truly, on a certain level, I was in the dark about their shared inner lives. They had their own fixed universe of values, my wife and children, their own intricate star charts and navigational devices evolved over thousands of intimate hours, and while I rolled in and out of that universe, a dependable satellite returning home each night, it was their planetary system, not mine.

When dinner was over, and I had done the dishes alone, I went down to the boys' room. From the other side of the door I could hear the muffled thumps of music. I knocked, and there was no answer. Instead of knocking again, I simply pushed open the door.

They were lying on their adjacent beds, indifferent to the rock and roll thundering from their boom box, playing with foot-tall robotic plastic superheroes called Bionicles. Will was holding Brutaka the warrior and Dwight was holding Nuva. They were tilted at forty-five-degree angles from each other, about six feet apart. As I watched, Dwight pressed a button on Nuva, and a small flying saucer wobbled through the air.

"I've got your Fantom disk on homing radar!" he cried.

"Yes," screamed Will in the faintly transistorized voice he used to speak Robot, "but you haven't reckoned with my handheld ion cannon!" He pressed a button and a tiny foam-tipped stick mostly fell from his Bionicle's shoulder.

"Who's winning, guys?" I cried, striding into the center of the room and turning down the stereo. I did a little boxing thing to break the ice, punching the air fast with both hands, and doing my modified Ali shuffle. Usually this draws at least a happy snort of laughter from the boys. But this time they both looked at me and then looked at each other.

"Hi, Dad," Will said levelly. Another glance crossed between them.

My potential rival might have been faceless, but no less

real for that. I could nearly feel him, suddenly, in the air of the room. In an adult voice I said, "No, go on, and play, boys, I just want to watch."

Without saying another word, both of them slowly put the toys down.

"What's wrong, guys? Go on and play, c'mon!" I picked up one of the small plastic robots, admiring the slickness of the manufacture, the smoothness of the injection molding, and remembering with a certain nostalgia the keyhole accuracy of the mind of childhood, when a single toy could exactly represent a whole world. Swallowing hard, I said, "Yo, dudes, why so quiet?"

They both stared at the ground, saying nothing. Finally, with a kind of sorrow, Dwight began to speak.

"Dad," he said, shaking his head, "the Bionicles cannot be interrupted during a final showdown."

"Daddy, we *told* you that. We told you," said Will.

"The Vanu-Grall rules say 'only uninterrupted battle.' Otherwise, it doesn't mean anything."

"It doesn't mean," echoed Will.

"Mean?" I asked.

"It's over," said Dwight, with an adult sigh of sadness. "We'd been fighting for a half hour and now it's no good."

"Oh, c'mon," I said, "that's just crazy."

"We'll have to start over, and now it's too late. Momma said we have to brush our teeth and go to bed. The planet Zamax is ruined."

They looked at each other, and as I slowly, even tenderly put the Bionicle back down on the bed in the silence, first Will, then Dwight, burst into tears.

The next day—a Saturday—I awoke determined to somehow address this feeling that the fine-grained sand of my own relationship with my children was slipping through my fingers. Was crazy old Shirley Castor right that boys come into the world for their mothers? We'd see about that. On the spot, I made the executive decision that I would take them to an indoor archery range. I broached the subject over breakfast—not asking, but telling Lucy in clear, calm terms that I was going to be taking the boys shooting. She looked at me with an alert flare of interest—not certain, I imagine, whether to be pleasantly surprised or suspicious.

Upper New York state, where we live, is a strange part of the world. A physically beautiful zone of valleys and rolling hills, it's also honeycombed with some of the most surprisingly redneck folks in the world. Monarch is a kind of spa in this setting, with its own civilized middle-class ambience, and its vaguely British commons and town square. Consulting the map, I noticed that the archery range was a half hour away, in a fairly wooded area I'd never been to before. I was a little bit concerned, but kept it to myself. Lucy waved good-bye from the door in perfect emulation of a happy spouse. It was only while I was backing the car out that I happened to glance at her again and saw the hard, etched, angry look come back over her face.

As we drove, my sons, indifferent to the looming domestic avalanche, made happy noises in the backseat. Sometimes I think all of boyhood can be reduced to lip, nose and hand noises. They were excited by the idea that they'd be shooting real weapons, and to keep them company, I tried to recall my own hunting bona fides. I did so by talking of that brief interval, about six months after my brother's death, when I was overcome by bloodlust, and took advantage of a pump-action BB gun to lay down a swath of murder from my parents' living room windows. At least a half-dozen times, I explained, I pressed the trigger, heard the spuft! of expelled air, and then rushed onto the back lawn and came upon the tiny body of a starling, still warm, blood beading on the breast feathers in minute duplication of its bright, fading eye. Then I sobbed, inconsolable. Then, seeing another bird fussing in the branches, I did it again. About a dozen times, I said, this same pattern repeated itself of prey ruthlessly hunted down, and then mourned with heartrending sorrow. After not too long, thankfully, this phase of life passed. "Boys," I said, "that was the end of one kind of hunting and the beginning of another, oh yes. I discovered girls, and nothing was ever the same. And you can bet your bottom dollar, hotshots, that the exact same thing will happen to you!"

For the second time in twenty-four hours, in response to a joking overture, my sons said nothing at all.

The archery range was called Into the Wild. It was a long, low Quonset hut–style building set deep in the woods. I followed the directions and then parked and shepherded the boys in the front door. A big surly-looking man in a buckskin jacket turned to face us at the cash register. "These little cowboys would like to do some shooting!" I cried, with far too much jocularity, as Dwight rolled his eyes, embarrassed. But the man behind the counter merely nodded, and said, "Sure thing. We'll get 'em suited up and on the range in a jiff."

"Dad," Dwight said disgustedly as we walked toward the range, "cowboys didn't shoot bows and arrows."

"They didn't shoot them," Will affirmed, shaking his head.

"Momma told somebody on the phone you're weird," said Dwight in a fierce whisper, and both the boys laughed deeply.

The range was lined with big rubber targets in the shape of animals, along with the more traditional bull's-eye targets set on huge rolling bales of some kind of plasticine packing material. When last I'd shot a bow and arrow, it was a simple curved piece of wood with a string, and the arrow a painted stick. But boys, even young boys, now use "compound" bows fitted with elaborate pulley and sighting systems, and carbon-fiber arrows designed specifically to cross space as fast as possible and impale themselves with terrifying impact. I was a little shocked—it was like discovering that box kites now came equipped with Hellfire missiles—but said nothing as the proprietor kindly fit the bows to the boys, and then showed them how to place their hands on the nock, or part of the string where they should pull the arrow back. "After firing your arrows, do not move until the word 'safe' is called, up and down the range, ya hear?" he asked them, squatting down to their height.

The boys nodded, solemn.

I sat behind them on a bench. I ate a mint and watched them emulating the derring-do of things glimpsed perhaps on television, or studied in their history classes, and as I did so I dwelled with a strange kind of relieved pride on our physical similarities. Will was identifiably my child, visually. The nose, the way the hair lay flat near the crown, the eye color, and more subtly, the walk and gait and slouch. Dwight, the younger, took more after Lucy, with her delicacy, her curling, dextrous fingers, her edge. He was the artist, clearly. And yet both of them had received from me those billions of genetic checks and twizzles that had produced a mimic cleft to the lower lip; an internal chemistry that affected the smell of their sweat and breath; an unnatural sensitivity toward light; and more subtly, a way of looking at the world, a slant, a struck chord, an essential lattice of identity.

I watched with joy in my heart, loving them their miniature replication of myself and the way their personalities expressed the differences thereof.

This buoyant feeling stayed with me all the way home. My elation, however, began to curdle fast as I watched the boys, at the entrance to the house, turn away from me, rush to Lucy, and, completely forgetting me in the process, begin overwhelming her with stories of the day; their valiant slaying of targets, the mythic heroism of it all. This sudden eruption of invisibility on my part was infuriating, and, it seemed to me, not accidental. Lucy would have told me that all this was entirely my doing, and the fruit of my own self-involvement of late, but I didn't buy it. She was clearly involved in my estrangement. I had submitted to the indignities of Purefoy. I had cooked and cleaned and come to her open armed and openhearted, in the spirit of reconciliation. But what she was doing now, as the boys yipped and hooted around her, and I looked on feeling my smile stiffening on my face, read to me as manipulative and nasty. I tried not to visit that particular salt lick of woundedness that, when touched, produced in me a fresh flare of outrage. I wanted, still, to plant love in the ground of my marriage. But when I looked at my wife, the certainty remained that she was showing pleasure not only in the attention paid her, but a joy as well in the knowledge that despite her husband's attempt at tilting the balance an inch the other way, the balance had remained entirely intact.

HOMICIDE TENDS TO MAKE RIPPLES IN THE human pond. Twenty-four hours after he'd committed murder, the first waves of Rob's act began to wash into our lives. It was the morning after our bender with him in New Russian Hall, and we were still drinking our coffee and massaging our pounding temples when the phone calls began to arrive, many of them mentioning that "something's up with Rob." They were from friends of friends who knew people who knew people. As the afternoon deepened, the calls turned more specific, and ominous. They were from someone's cousin who was a stringer for the AP who said there was a "buzz" about Rob. They were from a distant relative of the state police who had heard "bad stuff" about "that writer guy."

On the local afternoon news, the lead anchor opened with a quick national roundup, and then said, "A breaking story apparently involving one of Monarch's own, the writer Rob Castor. Monarch police chief Dick Striebel will be holding a press conference this afternoon, at four thirty, to be carried live, on this station." He then shook his head, as if in sadnesss, and threw it to the weatherman.

All over town, we sat back on our couches, stunned. This sudden ratcheting up of seriousness was too fast, too real, too *out there* in the public world to be easily digested. There was a confusion of velocity and scale between the gaunt, muttering person glimpsed the night before at New Russian Hall, and the blazoned event taking place a half day later on television. We called each other on the phone, confused, and spoke about the developing situation. Danger made us masculine, and in bursts of terse, bewildered feeling, we compared notes, and in the most elliptical terms possible admitted we felt strangely close in our shared distress.

Without ever exactly saying so, we all agreed we would watch the news conference together. And so, at about four P.M. that day, we began straggling in to New Russian Hall. It was the height of late summer and we wore flip-flops and cargo shorts. We dressed in loafers and khakis, and at least one of us in bib overalls with nothing underneath. We were men of early middle age in a confraternity of muddled feeling and hangover, concerned for a dear friend. Muted conversations rippled up and down the bar, having mainly to do with our regret, thinking back on it now, of not having been more solicitous of Rob the night before. We'd feted him as a great old pal of distinction. We'd piled on the accolades and bought him drinks. And yet in the interim since seeing him and hearing the rumors, nearly everyone had come to the conclusion that his subdued behavior was actually a sign of great distress, and that we should have recognized it, addressed it, somehow intervened. That knowledge made us sober. We ordered seltzer and prepared for the worst.

At four thirty sharp, the bartender, Freddie Rhoades, clicked off the Yankees game—engendering a single cry of protest from a liquored-up out-of-towner—and clicked on the news. The screen was bannered with glary bulletin motifs, and pulsed briefly with staccato danger music, and then the newscaster—our beloved local Lisa Langley—led into the press conference with a few sketchy sentences of background.

The screen quickly flashed to Chief Striebel. He was a balding older man who always looked a bit surprised by how badly he'd slept the night before. Into a silence broken only by the twitchy, repetitive sneezes of motorized cameras, he began to speak.

"I'm here to make a public announcement," he said, "in a fugitive case that concerns all of us. A former resident of Monarch, Robert James Castor, is currently wanted on suspicion-of-murder charges by the New York City police. Witnesses have placed him at a bar in Monarch last night, but he has not yet been apprehended. Due to the nature of this crime, and the fact that the man is a fugitive, the district attorney's office has asked that I go public and request the help of the people of Manateague County. This man is armed and dangerous and very motivated to avoid capture. If you see Rob Castor, do nothing. But contact your local law-enforcement authority immediately."

The screen then filled with a photograph of Rob—younger, beefier, radiant, and sharp looking—taken from his book jacket. He was posed in front of a tiger cage at the zoo, pointing somewhat subtly to the DON'T FEED THE ANIMALS sign.

A frenzied interrogatory baying of reporters was abruptly cut off as the screen filled again with Lisa Langley, sitting at the cramped local news desk. Back at the bar, we looked at each other, shook our heads and blew shocked air through our mouths. For a long moment, we were too surprised to speak and simply stared at the television. Somehow it seemed appropriate, nearly comforting, that it would be Lisa Langley delivering the bad news.

Lisa was a Monarch girl, a former high school classmate who had passed through the same rings of social fire as we and had gradually ascended (as we watched, proudly) the ladder from editor of the school paper all the way up to TV reporter on the nightly news. Her "beat" was local-color stories with a redemptive twist, and if over the years the flawless bone structure of her face had gradually gone round and maternal, and her lean frame filled with empathetic fat, then these elements were part of her essential wholesomeness. It was clear she'd never make it to the national markets, and with her curiously auntish hairdo would retire still softly announcing the latest strike at the Ulster Biscuit factory, or the direction of the shadow cast by Punxsutawney Phil. But that somehow only made us feel closer to her.

Now she was reshuffling the papers on her desk with light little taps; she was raising and lowering her head as if rehearsing the moment of starting to speak. We realized, suddenly, that she was emotionally overcome. Unable to resist the hypnotic suggestiveness of television, we became instantly overcome as well.

Then Ferd Nickles cried out, "Hold on! Hey! Don't you remember, they used to go out?"

There was a mutter of memory along the bar as we recalled, in fact, that they did go out, Rob and Lisa, and were briefly famous, in the electric territories of high school, for mixing Straight and Hip in such a manner as to elicit a hot wave of disapproval from both their sets of friends. It was, for that, one of those junior-year relationships whose fuck-you value considerably exceeded any affinity the principals might have had for each other.

Up on the screen, having recovered her self-control, Lisa said, "Rob Castor was an essential part of Monarch life. For those of us, like myself, who'd grown up with him, this is an especially sad moment." Then she looked directly into the camera, and for one thrilling and appalling moment we were certain she was going to address Rob directly. She seemed about to say something. But then the camera cut away to an aspirin commercial, and it was clear that the Rob coverage was over.

There was a sick, long sigh along the bar. I can't help but feel that in some way it was the definitive exhalation of the end of our youth. It's not an exaggeration to say we were different afterward; that some final veil forever slipped away from our faces and pitched us forward into a new smallness of vision, a sadder, more baleful take on life. Nearly all of us, I think, took the opportunity, after what we now knew, to train a more penetrating gaze on ourselves. We were not especially reflective, most of us. We prided ourselves on our unshakability. We liked it that way. The modern world was dangerous, squirrely, insidious and weird. Indifference was a firewall and detachment was a shield. The gift of Rob's act was to undermine all that and to toss our assumptions into a cocked hat, to start a meter running in each of us, whose ticking would accompany a newly mortal conception of our own selves. Speaking for myself, I can say that his death, although I didn't know it at the time, would be part of the beginning of my new life.

# chapter 20

"I'M DETECTING," SAID DR. PUREFOY smoothly, "a certain resentment on your part today."

"That could be," I admitted.

"Do you want to talk about it?" asked the doctor, resplendent in a sharkskin suit, an open-collared white shirt and tapering Italian shoes. It was our fifth session together, and the one, I'd already decided, in which I was going to make a clean break. I waited patiently for his long hands to be steepled together, doing my best to conceal the intensity of my pleasure when, after about ten seconds of fraught silence, his forefingers touched.

"I can try," I said. "I think I feel dissatisfied during these sessions, especially lately, because, well, in all candor, Doctor, they seem to me basically a waste of time and money. We're getting nowhere at all, at least from where I'm standing, and on top of that it's like there's some kind of subtle agreement between you and my wife that puts me at a disadvantage as soon as I walk in the door."

The doctor tapped his forefingers together in a gesture that signaled either thoughtfulness or applause while a single eyebrow, with astonishing independence from its twin, rose and then fell. "Disadvantage?" he asked. "What kind of disadvantage?"

"A kind of shadow suspicion, I guess: that I'm the real problem in this marriage, that I'm . . . either a liar or someone so emotionally bogged down as to be useless, and that I'm somehow not worthy of her finer feelings. That kind of disadvantage."

The doctor nodded as if expecting this and said, "Hmmm." After waiting a few seconds, he went on to say, slowly, as if marveling, "Very good, Nick. Very very good. Do we need a more obvious sign of the progress we're making than this new eruption of candor? Anger in these circumstances is good, it's honest, it's something to go on. In distinction to what you said a moment ago, I think we *are* getting somewhere, and I think your . . . aggression is proof of it. We're accessing those core truths you've been afraid to touch till now, and I applaud you, Nick, for what you just said and how you said it. I believe it signals a new clear channel of feeling between not only you and me but you and your wife as well."

Once, even a few months earlier, this would have been enough for me. I would have been too eager to please to contest it. But things were different now. I said, "Thanks for the appreciation, Doctor, but it doesn't change the fact that I just don't feel good in here. I feel I'm being subtly undermined by you, and I'd like to take this moment to tell you that I've decided to end my participation in these sessions. Of course, you two should feel free to . . . keep doing whatever you've been doing. But I'm opting out."

Dr. Purefoy had continued nodding encouragingly, even admiringly, I thought, while I spoke. But after I stopped, there was a long silence during which his face, with incredible subtlety, mainly around the eyes and mouth, grew cold. When his voice next came, it contained the specific tone of pitying condescension that had put my teeth on edge from our very first exchange many years earlier.

"I suppose you've never heard of the phenomenon of projection, have you, Nick?" he asked.

"Let me put it this way, Doc," I said calmly. "I think you've got a thing for my wife, and what I'd like to tell you is, if you need to talk to me about it man-to-man sometime, then that's okay."

Afterward, in the parking lot, Lucy was pale with rage.

"I despise you," she said, on the edge of tears, "and I'll never forgive you for what you just did."

"I'm sorry, honey, but I can't stand that guy. Your anger will pass."

"No it won't."

"Yes it will, and when it does, you'll understand that the reason you're pissed at your husband is because he crashed your little fantasy love boat."

"You're a loathsome man," she said.

"Stop it." I caught up to her and grabbed her sleeve.

"You really are ill." She shook me off, yanked open the car door, plunked herself violently down on the passenger seat and crossed her arms.

In response, I exaggerated the slowness and care with

which I opened my own door and sat myself down on the tufted seat.

"You do have a thing for him, admit it," I said in a throaty, pleasant voice, starting the car and putting it in gear. "Not that I blame you, understand. He's a handsome guy, and those fancy French shades he wears in his breast pocket alone must cost two hundred dollars, easy. I've never heard of a shrink who wears as many fancy clothes as this guy does, and in Monarch no less. Who does he analyze, Barbra Streisand?"

Staring out the window, she said slowly, "He told me you were fixated at the anal-sadistic stage, but I actually think you've begun regressing further back."

"Where to?" I was enjoying this exchange, in a peculiar fashion. "My mother's fallopian tubes? The thing that really gets me is the way you sit around in front of him with your tongue practically hanging out, and then write him a check for the privilege of having done so."

She turned to me.

"Thank you," she said, blotting her eyes with a tissue.

I nodded. "For what?"

"For making everything that's about to happen so much easier."

I drove the rest of the way home in silence, trying to tell myself I was glad that something, at least, had been broken open between us. This ebbing sense of triumph accompanied me through the rest of a glacial evening. All of this, I insisted to myself, plumping up the pillow and settling into a thin and dreamless sleep, was for the best. But the next day, without wanting to, and for the first time since marrying her, I abruptly entered into a phase of wondering what my wife was doing with all her late mornings and early afternoons. I'd never wondered before. I had always simply assumed she was engaged in her daily round of tasks and let it go at that. Over the years, my visual memory of Lucy had begun to fade a little bit from vividness, the detailed daily imagining giving way to a warmly abstract buzz.

But suddenly, for the first time in recent memory, I "saw" my wife. I saw the sexual composite of flat stomach, breasts, and fine nose, and I imagined her moving through the world with those qualities exposed to the eyes of passersby, and weirdly, uncontrollably, I found myself uneasy at that fact. I tried to turn the unease into the more reasoned state of indignation. I told myself that it was unnecessarily provocative that she still be firm and desirable and show it off with clothes that could have been looser, less shaped, more concealing of her essential form. I told myself that this was a kind of disloyalty on her part, and that she better shape up. I watched her in my mind's eye in line at the supermarket, and I found myself remembering the heavy, hanging open face of the butcher as he'd handed her her package of meat; how the traffic cop who'd stopped her for speeding had leaned in the window in a bizarre access of friendly intimidation and clearly ogled her breasts (and there was something fundamentally sick and twisted, anyway, about traffic cops giving tickets to women in cars and having licensed sanction to look down their shirts the while, wasn't there?); or the way a certain neighbor, when drunk at backyard garden parties, had let his whole head fall forward in admiration of Lucy, his mouth dropped lewdly open, his nose stuck out emphatically in the air in front of him in a way, I saw now, that most clearly resembled a penis.

The world was full of men trying to get women. What was there to prevent Lucy from tossing her pretty head and shattering the delicate marital enclosure in which she was (willingly) penned? When we'd gone to the sex club, hadn't she admitted to a kind of flush of excitement at seeing people doing it in public? The arousal of my wife, a fact that I'd worshipped over the years, also frightened me a little. I'd always depended on her self-control. And yet I knew that when moved to it, she was capable of orgasms far larger, more violent and engulfing than my dribbling evacuations. Once tapped, her desire was a forest fire, a force beyond her or anyone else's control. I thought I understood, now, why the Islamic world bridled and bitted its women with flowing tunics and darkened masks: because the female form is a nearly insane incitement to men. Tits and asses! Legs and pussies!

A strange new tic installed itself in my nervous system. It was a kind of swallow and retraction of the head, as if quizzically observing some piece of new information freshly alighted in the visual field. Driving my car to work, eating lunch with colleagues, I did the tic. I watched myself doing it. I didn't like it but I did it anyway. I was simply holding too much inside. I knew I was. Lucy was right that I'd always believed there was something "strong" about this kind of impassivity. She was correct that I'd always connected manliness with swallowing the nasty thrusts and cuts of life in silence. It was she, after all, who had told me after an earlier visit to Purefoy that I was "stuck in a classic male holding pattern" and added, straight-faced, that I needed to acquaint myself with "the adult pleasures of vulnerability."

Vulnerability, as it turns out, was not long in coming—although whose vulnerability remained to be seen. One afternoon, about a week after the last visit with Purefoy, the phone rang at work. The phone often rang at work. But rather than a peevish lab tech asking for a raise or a university professor pleading special consideration for a grad student, the voice on the other end was low, sultry, and thrillingly raw: "It's me."

"Belinda." My desk chair whiplashed forward with a squeak of springs. "Well, hi."

"Hey," she said, "how's life?"

"Life?" I looked around the room on reflex, startled, and then pivoted in the chair, extended a foot and toed the office door shut. "I'd give it a solid C plus."

"Too bad, but maybe this'll cheer you up."

"What's that?"

There was a pause. "I'm breaking up with Taunton," she said. Taunton was her spoiled rich-kid boyfriend.

"Tell me it ain't so!" I cried in mock anguish.

"Affirmative, Nick. When I met him he was a regular person with a job and a working set of balls, but ever since the inheritance kicked in, he does nothing but lie around the house buying things off eBay and having 'enthusiasms' about things. Do you have enthusiasms about things?"

"Rarely."

"That's what I love about you, Nick. From the beginning, it was clear you'd never amount to much, and that's been a huge comfort to me over the years."

Alone in my office, I suddenly relaxed in a way I hadn't in days and cracked a big smile. "Belinda."

"Hey," she said, and laughed.

I laughed too, deeply, and then said, "How nice to hear your voice."

"That's what friends are for, to quote that shitty song."

"Amen to that."

"Right, and now that I'm officially alone I'm feeling freshly freed up for other, uh, possibilities."

Blood stood up in my chest. In a casual tone of voice I said, "Cool."

"I'm glad we agree."

There was a pause. I felt the balance pans of the scale at the center of my marriage tremble, suddenly.

"So are you coming back soon?" I asked.

"Not soon enough. Curtis, out!" A dog barked, high and rapid, and then squealed as she kicked it with her foot.

"Actually," she went on, "that's why I'm calling."

"Yeah?"

"I'm coming back in four days, sugar, and I've got you penciled in—and underlined as well." She giggled.

"Well, great," I said.

"Yeah, I'll be home for about a month, and you know what?"

"What?"

"I just can't wait to see you, Nick."

"Can I let you in on a little secret?" I said, as one of the pans, now filled with engorged weight, dropped toward the bottom of its travel.

"Please do," she said.

"I feel exactly the same way."

## chapter 21

IN DISGUST, AS I WOULD LATER THINK OF it, at the deepening squalor of my private life, my father then had a heart attack. I'm not particularly mystical, but the timing of his event—on the same day as my phone call with Belinda—seemed to cry out for connection. Termed a "cardiac incident" by doctors, it was bad enough to put him in the hospital for several days. My mother told me the news in a voice pared to a single filament of exhaustion, and I made the snap decision—and paid a staggering ticket premium for my filial loyalty—to fly out there immediately in a show of support. As we taxied down the runway, I felt relief at rehearsing this literal movement up and away from the dark confusions of late, and when the plane reached cruising altitude, I ordered a vodka tonic as a hedge against my own anxiety. After a few minutes of staring out the window at America—from seven miles up an endless, rolling lichenous green plaque—I fell asleep.

It seemed only seconds later that the tires chirped and the plane shook me violently awake. My first thought was to ask for another drink, but then I looked out the window and saw the bright, irrefutable fact of Phoenix, Arizona. It was the longest I'd ever slept on a flight, and was evidence, clearly, that the recent domestic stresses were taking a toll.

The cab ride to Sunnyside Acres was half an hour, and for its duration, I lay back against the cushions, filled with premonitory dread and ignoring the washed-out desert tones of the landscape around me. I wanted to bolster my father in his moment of need. But I also wanted some questions answered. Against the live backdrop of my love for my sons, the deficiencies in my own upbringing seemed more glaring and inexplicable than ever. I shut my eyes a moment and, thinking about the boys, tried using our attachment as a prism through which to filter information about my own past.

Was one of my sons more obviously like me? Yes. And did that produce between us a more obviously clean channel of feeling? Yes, but only slightly. Was that enough to push the other so utterly outside the inner circle of charmed attention that he felt he'd been chuted into their lives like an errant air-mail?

Absolutely not.

Eventually we turned off the highway and not long after were curving through the grandiose entrance to Sunnyside. In the distance, hundreds of identical cute bungalow-style "villas" dotted a landscaped series of slightly convex hills, looking at a glance like jacks in the palm of a huge hand. Amid these were the elderly, in every variant of stooped, leaning, pitched and wobbly, congregated in the patches of shade beneath trees. The only time they moved quickly, my mother told me, was when exposed to the direct, killing rays of the sun. The irony was not lost on me that the very thing they worshipped and adored from behind double-paned windows was precisely that thing they feared most. I paid the cabbie, and with a beating heart, stepped to my parents' front door and rang the bell. The door swung open.

"Nick!" My mother leaned forward, embracing me in a crush of flesh and lilac powder. Behind her I had a dim impression of darkened space. They kept the blinds closed at nearly all hours.

I stepped inside. The house was tidy, spruce, miniature. A slant roof gave the living room a faintly Alpine impression. I spied my father near the modular sofa. Back from the hospital only the day before and wearing baby blue pajamas, he had been installed in an easy chair in a kind of levee of towels and pillows. Instead of getting up, he stared coolly at me.

"So, you're here," he said. "Hello, son."

"Hello, Dad."

I put my rolling bag down.

"Whyn't you come over here," he said. I crossed the room to him and when I leaned forward, he craned upward and in a vaguely papal way, rested his hand on my shoulder a minute. In a moment of reduced expectations, this would have to suffice as greeting. I pulled back and stared at him, the public voice in my head saying, "He looks well." But I did not utter those words.

"How are you, Dad?" I said.

He nodded, slowly.

"I've been better."

I tried to smile. "You took quite a shot, it sounds like."

"Nick, it was a little like being clubbed to death from inside your own chest."

I sat down on the couch, and took in the age-mineralized features, the defensive ice in the eyes, the big nose and the fleshy lips. The lips opened.

"You look like hell," he said.

"Lawrence, stop it," said my mother, sitting down across from us and smoothing her dress. I felt her scrutinizing gaze against the side of my face.

"You do look a little underslept," she said softly.

"That's because I am," I said.

"Aren't we all," said my father.

"Would you like something to eat or drink?" she asked.

"No, not quite yet."

There was a pause while it was borne in on me that none of us knew quite what to say. My relationship with my parents had been conducted intermittently and by phone for so many years that in the face of my actual, physical presence, we were all a bit self-conscious.

"What's the prognosis?" I asked.

"Bed rest," said my father, "some pills, as little fun as is humanly possible, and maybe I'll scrape by."

"What your father means"—my mother's lips drew down into a disapproving crimp—"is no drinking."

"Verboten, sonny," said my father. "The end of joy in life. From here on in, when I wake up in the morning, that's as good as I'll feel all day."

"It was a warning shot," my mother said, "what happened."

"I doubt it'll be that bad," I said.

"Doubt all you want," said my father. "It will."

He leaned back on his green Barcalounger. "But enough of all that. Tell us something good, Nick."

I paused before the breadth of possible answers, and decided to stick with a safe response. "Well, the boys and I went to shoot bows and arrows recently. That was fun."

"Ah, and how are the boys?" asked my mother, eager to reenter the conversation on solid ground.

"Fine."

"And Lucy?"

"The same as ever," I said.

"What's that mean," my father said, "her heart still beats, her eyes still open and shut?"

"Lawrence," said my mother, "stop it."

"I don't mind you asking, Dad. Things are okay at home, but sometimes I feel that I don't do enough with the boys."

"But why would you say that?" she asked. "You're a very good father."

"Am I? It seems to me there are so many ways to be a bad father that it can be a bit overwhelming. Sometimes I think that for mothers it's easier. They have a kind of genetic playbook on how to be with their children. But the fathers are always improvising, making up ways to build bridges to their kids. Does that make sense?"

"Yes," my mother said.

"No," said my father. "'Bridges to their kids'? What are you, in some kind of men's support group now?"

"Lawrence," my mother said again.

"Actually," I said, "on certain days I think I'd find the idea of a support group like that appealing."

Weakly, my father blew derisive air through his nose as my mother stood up.

"I've got a cold tuna casserole and I'm just going to whip up some salad. Does that sound good to you, Nicky?"

"Great, Mom."

She went into the kitchen while my father and I sat in stolid silence for several long moments, interrupted by my mother's return with a tray of heaped appetizers and drinks. Dinner, following promptly thereafter, was a strained attempt at high-heartedness, and the return to a kind of willful gaiety I remembered all too well from the years after Patrick's death, when at my birthday parties in particular, a rotely festive atmosphere reigned.

We were all exhausted, and went to bed early. I slept badly, on the rippled mattress in the guest room. The next morning, having forgotten to shut the blinds, I was awakened early by a shaft of sun in my face. My mother was still asleep. But my father, to my surprise, was already sitting in the easy chair, wearing a pained, somewhat weary expression. I entered the room quietly, still in my pajamas, and acknowledged him with a tentative smile.

"How are you feeling, Dad?"

"Groggy, thanks."

"Can I get you anything?"

"No, I'm fine for now."

I approached the lounge chair, and sat on the couch. There was a moment of silence, while both of us stared at the louvers of the main patio window beyond which the watered green backyard staked a brave, wavering claim against the desert.

"I've always loved the morning," he said quietly.

"Really?" I said encouragingly. "Why's that?"

"You know, when everything's shining, and nothing's happened, and the whole day is just waiting for you to go forward into it? It could be a lottery-winning day, it could be a completely average day, but you don't know yet, and that's part of what's so special about it. It's like every animal, when it opens its eyes, probably has that same morning moment."

I was touched by the vein of poetry suddenly opened up in this normally dry pragmatic man. I'd have liked to encourage it, but I knew that in only a few minutes my mother would wake and we'd be returned to our more formal triangulation, and I had some questions I wanted answered. I said, "That's nice, Dad, that you appreciate that. But can I talk to you a second about something else?"

"Of course."

"What it is," I said, "is the stuff that came up in that phone call we had recently."

"What's that, son?" He turned toward me with a smile.

"You know, about childhood and Patrick?"

I watched the smile crumple from the inside out. "That again?" he said "You came all the way down here to tell me you're still upset about something I said to you on the beach thirty years ago? Nick, please, I'm not supposed to laugh, it's bad for my heart."

I swiveled my gaze away from him, and stared at the wall, holding the image of the kind of candor I wanted in front of me. I addressed that candor, saying slowly, "What it is,

Dad, is that I'm going through a difficult phase right now, and I'm trying to get clear about things, and one of the things that keeps coming up is the disproportion between the way you treated me and the way you treated Patrick and the cold kind of arm's-length feeling I had, growing up. Over these last few months it's been preying on me, I don't know why. Not to beat a dead horse, especially now, with you being sick, but if we could talk about it a little bit—if we could clear the air and dispose of it once and for all, that would be a very good thing."

My father looked at me—really looked at me—for what seemed the very first time since I'd arrived. I was amazed to see how, within the rather washed-out territories of his face, his eyes were full, rich, shining.

"Your mother said there was some difficulty at home. Is *that* what all this is about?"

"No, yes, I don't know."

"What's going on there?"

I shrugged my shoulders. "Honestly, I don't know, but this is not a great period."

"How bad is it?"

"I think we may be separating."

"Christ," he said. "Really?"

Another silence.

"I hope not, but maybe. But you know," I began, "I'd still like to discuss this other—"

"Pardon my asking," my father interrupted, "but do you still love each other?"

"Love?" I said, and felt some formless thing shift under the surface of my skin. "Yes," I said slowly, "I think I do still love her. I still find her attractive. I still enjoy her

company, and feel some kind of gratefulness . . . for everything."

"Then what is it?"

Gently, persistently, cunningly, my father continued to
deflect my inquiries. It felt bad enough to be bringing up
this ancient material at all, especially given his condition.
Worse still was that he ignored it.

"What is it?" he asked again.

"I'd be lying if I told you I knew," I said. "She claims
that I'm absent lately, simply not there, stuff like that.
But"—again I shrugged my shoulders—"I don't know.
She's gotten insanely jealous recently as well."

He cleared his throat.

"Well, it's never easy," he said in a low voice.

"What?"

"Marriage."

"Don't I know."

He cast his eyes once around the room. "Do you? In my
day, there was no alternative to it. You didn't 'live together.'
You didn't have a 'summer of love' in your pajamas. No,
you tied the knot, and if it was a hangman's noose, well,
tough titty on you because you didn't even *think* about slipping it. But nowadays, what's marriage? Kleenex is what.
So it didn't work? You wad it up and throw it out. Come
here."

I picked up my chair and crab-walked over to him, sitting down close. He beckoned me closer, and as I leaned
toward him I noticed the faint, sourly fleeting aroma of the
hospital. "I'm only human, you think there weren't times
I wasn't distracted in my marriage to your mother? I was
gone, AWOL, somewhere else entirely, and for years too.

We passed a good long time in the deep freeze together, your mother and I, and sometimes I regret it, but not for me, for her," said my pale, drained father, recently granted a reprieve from the grave, and in the wake of it, unnaturally eager to talk about his feelings. "I regret she didn't get more of what she needed from me. Look, if you want your wife, you can find a way to keep her. She's your wife, for Chrissake. And if it's her happiness you're after then you gotta"—incredibly, he slowly waggled his hips under the bathrobe—"make her happy by wooing her a little, if you get my drift. Make nice with her in bed, and cozy up."

Where had the autocratic cold father of my childhood gone? For a moment, this barrage of deathbed sincerities almost made me miss him.

"Thanks, Dad."

"Life is short. Concentrate on the essentials," he said.

"Right."

"Breakfast is served!" announced my mother, mysteriously appearing at the living room door; I hadn't even heard her wake up. "To the table, gentlemen!" she cried, in a voice that mimicked the sound of happiness but was drained of it. Obviously, this line of conversation with my father would have to wait. We had returned to our more formal configuration of three, and I sensed (correctly, as it turns out) that I wouldn't get another chance to be alone with him before I left. On the heels of that perception, getting to my feet to eat, a deep deflation swept over me. Not that this deflation was shared by other members of the family. "Take her to bed and remind her of who you are," whispered my merry, heartsick father, rising from the vault of his sea green lounger like a submarine.

# chapter 22

BELINDA AND I MET AT A MUTUALLY agreed upon place a couple of towns away from Monarch, a restaurant, dark and lamplit, a snuggery out of the cold, perfect for adulterers. Arriving first, I sat down in one of the plush booths, and in the few minutes before she got there, I did my very best to remain on the guilt-free train of logic that I'd boarded that morning upon waking up: that it was somehow circumstance, not me, that was bringing this to pass; that there was a way in which life itself had assumed control of things with a heavy, blue-balled inevitability; that for the sake of decency, if nothing else, I should step aside, and let the world—so apparently interested in unzipping my fly—have its way. I loved my wife. But I was also (recalling my anthropology classes from college) a hominid, and a descendant of clubbing, tearing, hacking creatures, who fanged meat and broke open skulls. As such, perhaps the crimped daintiness of monogamy was simply against my nature, and maybe, for that, even a crime against the state.

I ordered a Bloody Mary out of solidarity with my inner ape, and drank it quickly. It went straight to my head, of course, because I normally don't drink vodka at lunch. Feeling faintly defiant and exhilarated, I was just finishing the drink when Belinda entered at the far side of the restaurant and proceeded toward me at a casual saunter. She was wearing heels, which flexed her diamond-shaped calves, and black stockings laddering into a short tight skirt that in turn debouched upward into a black top, fitted to underscore the heft of her breasts. It was an emphatic entrance, declaratory like a shout, and my head, already weighted with alcohol, fell slightly forward in disbelief.

"Well, wow," I said, getting to my feet and bending to kiss her. She displaced any doubts I had about the purpose of our encounter by ignoring my inclined, politely pursed lips and pulling me toward her into a three-point stance of breasts, lips and cocked pelvis. Lucy was delicately made, but Belinda was built like a beautiful nose tackle, with all her physical features outsized, as if for the anatomically hard of hearing.

"Hi there," she said casually.

"You look absolutely fantastic," I said.

"Do I?" Her voice was low, and standing inches away from me, she let her arms linger around my neck. "I just threw on whatever I could find."

"Somehow," I said, smiling back at her, "I don't think so."

With a wink, she detached her arms from me and seated herself on the other side of the table. I heard the lisp of fabric as she crossed her stockinged legs, and in that split second felt my previously guiltless locomotive derailed on the spot. Who was I kidding? Belinda radiated sex. There was no way to look at her and think that what would ensue when a few drinks were added to the mix would be casual, or a surprise. I had configured the lunch in my mind as a series of glancing impacts, which even if they landed us in the sack would do so as a result of something plausibly approaching coincidence, but the sexual clarity of her intent and voice worked against that. I grew slightly uneasy as I realized there would be no shirking responsibility for whatever happened. I had held to that shred of moral high ground and now it was removed.

"I see you couldn't wait," she said, and smiled as she nodded at the empty glass in front of me. She seemed to take it as a tribute of sorts.

"I've got a lot on my mind," I said.

"Really, such as?"

"Can I get you a drink?"

"Yes, white wine."

"Excuse me?" I snagged a passing waiter and placed the order as she put her bag on the table, and did the back-flexing thing, her breasts rearing.

"So," she said, falling forward again. "How we doing, friend?"

"*We* are doing fine," I said, emphasizing the pronoun. "It's the *I* I'm worrried about."

I laughed nervously in the silence.

"Really?" she asked. "What's up?"

I hadn't wanted to lead with my difficulties. This kind

of conversational tack was against my nature. Maybe it was the vodka. I said, "No, nothing, just the usual stress of life, I guess."

She looked at me, her head canted off slightly to one side in doubt, studying me. "God, I really do know you, Nick," she said. "I know and know and know."

"Really?" I asked, relishing the sensual innuendo of her phrasing. "Whattya know?"

"I know that you were a perfect, polite little child and you've become an unnaturally controlled guy." Her hand began to crawl toward mine over the tablecloth. "I know you've got 'stewardess-face,' and you always have. You can't stop looking composed even as your life is catching fire and burning to death at thirty-five thousand feet." Her hand now reached mine with a small electric touch, and I started.

"Whyn't you let a little air out of those tires, honey?" she asked in her low voice as we both laughed, and her hand, lying on mine, suddenly tightened.

"I've got an idea," she said.

"Why am I suddenly nervous?"

"Let's play twenty questions."

"Oh, c'mon."

"Twenty questions, Nick. It'll be a great way to catch up."

"Okay." I shrugged my shoulders. "Whatever, sure."

"Great, I'll start. Swing set in the backyard?"

"Uh," I said, catching on after a second, "do you mean do we have one? Yeah, we have a—"

"Wooden fruit bowl on kitchen table?"

"In fact, yes."

"Ethan Allen in the living room?"

"Philippe Starck from Target, actually."

"When's the last time you were happy to feel your wife's hand on your arm?"

"No comment."

"Xbox for the kids?"

"Yes," I admitted.

"Do you dream of sex with old girlfriends?"

"It's been known to happen."

"Basement workshop?"

"A small one."

"Riding mower?"

"Jesus, self-propelled."

"Netflix?"

"Blockbuster."

"Have you ever," she asked, leaning back in such a way as to subtly cantilever her breasts into my line of sight, "had a screamin' hot dream about me?"

"Good evening," interrupted the resonantly self-conscious voice of the waiter, "might I inform you of tonight's specials?"

Both of us turned to look, each struggling in a different way not to burst out laughing, and listened as he recited the entrées with the special overemphatic pronunciation of servers in pretentious restaurants. I ordered the steak and *pommes frites.* She got *pasta puttanesca.* Together, we ordered the wine.

"To answer your question," I said, after the waiter had left, "yes."

"Yes what?"

"About you. Yes, I have."

"Dreamed?"

"That's right, I admit it."

"Well, you're not the only one," she said in her low voice, and squeezed my hand again and winked.

Over the next few minutes, gliding on our previously established mood, we effortlessly deepened the terms of our understanding. We would be partners of a sort, complicit in the larger enterprise of pretending we weren't deeply attracted to each other, and as part of that pretense, we would talk our heads off. We would court each other, in other words, as if the outcome wasn't preordained. It had been a long time since I'd actually unburdened myself like this, chattering away in widening circles of affinity about the things that moved me, the things that disgusted me, the things that made me want to take risks in life and jump off a cliff into unknown worlds. The food came. We ate—I discovered I had a huge appetite—and we drank, the mood unwinding further, and for many minutes at a time, I was able to forget the issues that had lately been pushing into me and clamoring for attention. For whole stretches I was simply aloft on the buoyancy between us. She was chatty, affectionate, girlish, flirty. Then she was blustering, hard charging, outlandish and foul mouthed. At a certain point toward the end of the lunch, with the great windblown feeling of hilarity still moving through the room, she suddenly said, "And forgive me for asking, but how's the sex with Lucy?"

The wind, abruptly, slackened.

"C'mon, Belinda," I said, dispirited even to hear my wife's name mentioned.

"No, really, is it make-up sex, or real sex?"

I lowered my eyes to the table.

"Is it sex out of wanting her, Nick?" she persisted. "Or as compensation for having hurt her feelings?"

Sometimes, when Belinda was like this, what I mainly felt was stalled and thick. It was a shutdown that arrived, unreconstructed, from all the way back in adolescence, and the conversion of my failure at being charismatic with girls into the labor-intensive option of "becoming friends." I could hear the familiar chain-dragging hesitancies of that time in my mind now as I raised my eyes and stared at her, uncertain how to respond. Why couldn't I ever simply lift myself up and rush straight at what I wanted to say, like Rob always did—or Belinda too for that matter?

As if sensing my loss of momentum, she leaned over her plate, holding her bottom lip in her teeth, and then she smiled a special smile. It was a smile that forgave all; that promised me a complete and total pardon in advance of anything I might say. I was dazzled by the implications of that smile. "Have you ever fucked a woman against a wall in the back of a restaurant, Nick?" she asked softly.

Staring at me for a long moment, she gently put down her knife and fork, placed her napkin on the table and got slowly to her feet. As she did so a wave of bridling air seemed to pass upward over her like a hoop that rose from the ground and finished, glistening, at her hair.

"Nick," she said, smiling, "I'm heading to the bathroom here. I know this bathroom. It's dark and it's got scented candles. I'm going to be there for at least five minutes. And if there should be a knock on that locked bathroom door, I'm going to open it."

I watched her walking away, the cheeks of her ass kneading the shiny material of her skirt, and I felt, as I have for at least twenty years, the human shadow that falls between the disembodied function of admiration and the carnal fact of the man who stands up and drops his pants. I could have spent all day relishing her good looks. I could have even gotten aroused doing that relishing. But I couldn't—not yet anyway—have simply pulled the trigger and acted on what I saw.

Fittingly, instead, I slowly shut my eyes, and for a moment, hiding in the darkness, I paged backward in time through my own encyclopedia of sex. I remembered the orthopedic contortions in the backs of cars, the incredible quiet wars of attrition with young girls, the sticky joys and feverish pounding heats of the high school years, and the long, slow-motion erotic decline of my marriage. In that moment I saw how much of my life had been drawn up around somehow minimizing the knowledge of that marital disappointment. I'd deployed the numbing pleasures of routine. I'd circled the wagons of children, house, the job and the hollow joys of consumption. I'd lulled myself to sleep with stories of the success of my "maturity" and its attendant dull buzz of early middle age. And it had almost worked. Almost, that is, I'd forgotten there were alternatives to sensual shutdown, and steadily decreasing erotic returns. Almost, I had gotten away with it. Yet a loophole had remained, leading back into that original fever dream. And Belinda Castor had just slithered through that loophole in a rush of silky fabric, high heels and innuendo. Eyes closed, I remained sitting very still, trying unsuccessfully to think my way through to a decision on what to do next. This sense of willful inertia was depressingly familiar. When I heard a noise and opened my eyes, she was coming out of the bathroom. I steeled myself for an angry or at least disappointed woman. And yet when I saw that rather than being angry with me, she was smiling and at ease—it was then (characteristically!), in the wake of being absolved, that I grew hard in my pants.

"My cautious pal," she said, sitting herself back down and sipping her wine.

"A pleasure deferred," I said, and then heard myself to my surprise say, "but not for long, I hope."

She looked at me, her smile widening. "I can work with that," she said, and under the table took my knee between her two knees, and began rubbing on both sides with the stockinged insides of her leg in such a way that a delicious shiver, beginning seemingly at the soles of my feet, rippled all the way up my spine.

An hour later, in her hotel room, when I was finally inside her, and blotted out by the whiteness of sex, I managed for a while to forget everything. White the room, white the neural roar inside my body as I fell repeatedly into her, and thought *this* is what I wanted, and *this* is what I needed. Then the bigger engines of sex themselves began to turn over, and the "I" faded, and suddenly, as happens occasionally, the sex began having *us*; the machine of sex with its nozzles and sprockets and flailing levers carrying us both forward, as if we were crossing a literal distance, rowing hard.

When it was over, for a few seconds, everything was sparkling, saline, rinsed clean by the solvent action of what had happened.

"Oh, Belinda," I said.

"You see"—she laughed a little laugh—"I told you."

"You did."

"And you didn't believe me."

"I didn't."

"That it could be this good and easy and hot."

"And loving."

She turned toward me in bed, her face rubbed clean of makeup by our greedy kissing, her eyes filled with a strangely candid light.

"And loving," she said.

It was that word. It was that silly word. It rattled around inside me like a stick banging a radiator. It went straight from my brain down to my heart, which grew literally fat with feeling. I got hard again.

"Oh, my," she said, looking down. "I do love a hungry man."

# chapter 23

I AM NOT AND HAVE NEVER BEEN ESPE-
cially religious. When very young, Christianity to me was
a vast, remote armamentarium of punishments so extrava-
gantly drastic as to need only be hinted at to be effective.
Hell was a useful concept for many years, but was eventually discarded at adolescence, with Rob's help, in favor
of infinity. How could there be superheated regions of
the damned when all but a tiny fraction of the universe
was empty space, and amid those trillions of void miles,
only the occasional mineral lump of a planet or the fizzing
furnace of a star to break the monotony of it all? Empti-
ness, not content, was the true message of life, and "good
works" and "Christian charity," it was clear, were piffling
human constructions when faced with the facts of deep
time and interstellar space.

Yet, as scattershot as it was, my religious training had
evidently left its mark, because in the days after my tryst

with Belinda, I spent a lot of time confidently awaiting retribution in the most time-honored Christian fashion. Would it arrive as a tragic report from the pediatrician, or the surprise surfacing of some ruinous forgotten debt? Would Lucy, recently grown a touch warmer with me out of compassion for my father, turn on me in a sudden homicidal fury and stab me in the eye, or my colleagues on the job solemnly open my office door and explain to me that my services, after all, were no longer required?

Instead of any of that, as it turned out, nothing happened. My car didn't spring a sudden flat and send me cartwheeling into oblivion. My house wasn't struck by a meteorite, nor was I, like the famous farmer in France, brained in the middle of a field by a compacted mass of frozen airliner effluent, and killed. My sleep wasn't any worse. If anything, it was better.

And yet as time went on the happy sated feeling in my nerves gradually gave way to a strange, helpless openness, in which I felt myself increasingly becalmed in life. It was as if I were on the receiving end of some mysterious large process, and singled out for special attention. *The world knew*, I told myself. The world knew what I'd done and the world was taking action. And part of that action was to make sure that it—the world—perforated me so violently with its sights and sounds that I was paralyzed out of sheer nervous saturation. I grew weirdly sensitive to human suffering in this period, and strangely, easily moved to tears by stories of mine collapse, of the death of horses by wildfire, of persistent coma victims waking up suddenly and embracing loved ones. I walked around looking for stories of violent redemption, of eleventh hour pardons and charismatic reconciliations. And my guilty gift to Lucy was to gaze at her across the gulf of our estrangement with eyes that saw only her benevolence. Regret is a dazzling cosmetic. As was the case previously when I'd kissed Belinda but now even more powerfully, I was blinded by the light of her calmness, her patience, the untroubled simplicities of her heart.

I fought back against my remorse by citing to myself the fact that nearly 40 percent of men commit adultery. I told myself, changing tack, that my home life was a wounded animal and I'd given it a merciful pistol shot to the skull. I pled the case that I was simply self-soothing, getting my own needs met and blowing off some steam, the better to return to my loved ones refreshed in spirit. These speeches were eloquent; they were persuasive. For a while, they worked to stave off the inevitable. But one morning the sun rose on the edifice of my marriage and showed me a lovely church now desecrated with adolescent rage, and the union upon which I'd gazed indifferently for so many months somehow mystically transfigured into a model of intelligent coexistence, and I knew then that it was over, and that I had lost.

I'd surrendered to the stupidest, most shallow, most idiotic slavery of them all: sex.

All of these conclusions were entirely internal, of course. No one knew my feelings. I'd been living with secrets for long enough that I'd actually gotten the knack of it. And relations at home with Lucy were so withered that she wouldn't have noticed my subtle changes in mood and feeling unless I'd shouted them out loud. My heart might have ached, but my face reflected the same potted geniality as ever. When one morning around this time, a cracked, vaguely familiar female voice called at work, I said nothing at all in response to its hello. Even though I couldn't place the voice, I associated it intuitively with trouble, and I had more than enough trouble in my life at the moment. I hoped the voice would go away. But it didn't go away. "Don't you recognize me?" the voice asked. "This is Shirley Castor and it's urgent that I see you today."

I'd almost forgotten about Shirley Castor. After my last visit to her months earlier, I'd been so disgusted by her drunken cruelty that I'd done my very best, even while lying on top of her daughter, to forget she'd ever drawn breath. But now she was croaking excitedly in my ear that she had "important information" to impart to me, and that it was "top secret" to boot. Deeply suspicious, I nonetheless told her yes, I'd be there, begged off the usual deli lunch with colleagues, and drove over that day. I feared the worst. I hadn't talked to Belinda in the interim aside from a brief, warm, exclamation-filled e-mail exchange, but I was certain that Shirley knew about the liaison. In the absence of knowledge, I revolved imagined Belinda scenarios of blackmail, pregnancy, suicide attempt or worse.

I arrived, parked and approached the house, pushing through deep snow while noting that the only visible tracks in the otherwise inviolate slab of white on her lawn were those of the mailman—probably delivering circulars—which led out to the place he parked his truck. Clearly, no car had been there, which led me to wonder if she'd been living on cat food since the snowfall had hit, several days earlier.

This time, ringing the front bell, there were no teenage

memories of erections under a sunny attic roof. Clearly, something far more serious was in the offing, and as if in confirmation, she met me at the door deliberately toned down, wearing only a drab housecoat, her hair in dry snarls and her face, unsprung by the upward tug of makeup, hanging creased and slack. A cigarette was fixed in her hand. Even though it was only noon, her eyes were unfocused. "Brrr," she said, opening the door. "Hurry in!"

I leaned forward in an uncertain gesture of amiably general greeting, but she turned her body sharply away from me and shunted me to one side, where I kept moving forward into the dark, stale air of the home. She pirouetted to follow.

"Cold enough for you?" she said.

"Sure is, but I'm bundled up pretty good."

"Isn't that nice."

She motioned irritably with her chin toward the living room and I slid past her, seating myself on the creaking slipcovered sofa. She sat in a chair across from me, and looked me slowly up and down.

"Well, well, well," she said, stubbing out her cigarette and leaning back and folding her arms on her skinny chest, "if it isn't Mr. Nicholas Framingham."

I nodded stiffly.

"An old English name, Framingham," she went on.

Again I nodded.

"An illustrious name," she added.

This time my nod was barely perceptible.

"But then again, what's in a name, right?"

As I watched, she lit another cigarette with a series of tired fluent gestures.

"Mrs. Castor," I said, but she held up a hand to stop me.

"I know," she said. "Be patient."

She reached down alongside the chair and raised up the familiar yellow canister, from which she took a long drink.

"I'm gonna tell you the truth about something that has been with me for over thirty years. I'm gonna do it because, well, I can, and because I'm tired. On top of that, in case you haven't noticed, I'm old. I wasn't supposed to be old, but it happened anyway. It's time to clear my debts. And one of my debts is to you, Mr. Nicholas Framingham."

I felt my brow furrow.

"It was a bad thing that happened all those years ago, and I was always certain that it was nearly a victimless crime, but it wasn't. Of course people do adapt," she said. "In the Indian town of Ahmedabad I once saw a dozen cripples with stick legs and withered arms—not moping, but dancing! It's not what you're given in life, it's what you do with it that counts, eh?"

I was by now totally bewildered.

"It hurt me, it hurt her, it hurt just about everybody, but they adapted, oh yes they did."

I could no longer keep silent.

"Who adapted, Mrs. Castor?"

"Your parents," she said.

I felt a sudden constriction in my throat.

"And to what did they adapt?" I asked with a certain effort.

She took another swallow from her canister and ate another puff of cigarette smoke.

"How are you, Nick?" she asked.

"I thought I was fine until about ten seconds ago. Is there something I should know?"

"Thirty-some years ago," she said, "I was called back to San Francisco on urgent business. It was an incredibly hot summer and people were outside on their lawns constantly, wearing as few clothes as possible. The sun is a hot, lecherous and even disgusting thing. In controlled doses, I believe it can make people quite crazy. Do you agree?"

"Uh, actually, I'm not sure."

"Really? That's too bad. Trust me, it can."

"Okay," I said, "so it can."

"And it did, in this case."

"In which case, Mrs. Castor?"

"Friend," she sighed, sat back in her chair, and took another drink, "here's the way I see it. I'm going to die soon. Die. And I'd like to have a clean slate before I go. Do you understand?"

Slowly, doing my best to encourage her, I nodded.

"That's why I invited you here. I want to travel to that afterlife as lightly as possible, even if"—her eyes rose to meet mine—"they say it's a long trip."

She smiled, horribly.

"What is it you wanted to tell me?" I asked.

"A secret," she said, "a nice fat juicy one. Not that I mind keeping secrets, understand. Secrets," she pronounced, "are the salt and pepper of life. Did you know that's one of my lines? I wanted to be a writer. No, strike that"—she grinned—"it was expected that I *be* a writer—by my father of course. A terrible man, my daddy, in the line of some kind of Romanoff merchant prince in his own mind. Do you know of the Romanoffs, you poor dim boy?"

Despite the hour of the day, it was clear she was dead drunk.

"What is it you wanted to tell me?" I repeated.

"Oh, lots," she said gaily, and lit another cigarette with the burning end of the first. She was still inhaling when the heater suddenly kicked in with a distant whooshing sound, and the rush of warm dry air brought with it that special yeasty, bone-deep funk of metabolized booze and cigarettes that attaches only to a special class of miserably cross-addicted people. I felt a faint twinge of nausea, and coughed into a hand.

"Why do you think it was my son met that awful girl?" she asked. "He was so utterly unprepared for that kind of woman."

It took a few seconds of swallowing before the nausea passed.

"Which woman was that?"

"That horrible Kate Pierce. A wolf is what she was, a wolf dressed like a lamb." She shook her head in disgusted recollection. "I'll never forget the first time I met her. Her fangs were just little stubs then. You could barely see them. But I could feel the corruption coming off her. That Little Bo Peep act didn't fool me for one minute."

"Mrs. Castor," I said.

"A woman," she ignored me, "can corrupt a tender-hearted man in a flash, Nick. She can put a hex on him as easily as pouring herself a glass of water, and ruin his virility. Soon, she overturns his heart, and she fogs his brain too. You think it's so hard? Men," she said scornfully, "are all full of bragging wind when seen from the front, but just reach around"—her long knobbed hand paddled the air, and snapped shut—"and open them up from behind and you'll find a little on/off switch, wired directly to their little egos. The funny thing is"—she gave a phlegmy cough into her folded fingers—"it's undefended! Oh yes, buried behind the career and the drive is that little-boy switch, that little red button, and you just give it a little flip, and the lion becomes a cooing, silly dove in about one hot minute."

She leaned forward, and toggled an invisible switch in the air. The bitterness in her voice was deep, ancient.

"Flip-flop," she said, and drank deeply from her canister. "Rub-a-dub-dub, away in your tub, Mr. Accountant, Mr. Executive, Mr. Millionaire Athlete. Go play with your ducky, Mr. Politician, Mr. Race Car Driver. You men," she sniffed, mainly to herself, as if in commiseration with some inner voice, "are all such hot air and little-boy bullshit."

She stopped, and lifted her eyes over my head. "I hated Marc so much," she said quietly, mainly to herself, "that it's a wonder he lasted as long as he did. It's a wonder he didn't die earlier from my simply wanting him that way, dead."

She lowered her eyes to mine, and repeated the word with heavy emphasis.

"Dead."

"Mrs. Castor," I said again.

"At least he was handsome," she went on. "Oh, yes, with that cleft chin and the oiled Valentino hair—who was handsomer than he was? I saw him on the tennis court, and his legs, and those shorts—well, I was a goner on the spot."

She laughed merrily to herself a second. "What crazy kids we were! My father was against the marriage, of course. But when your whole life has been business, you want something better for your children than another number cruncher, sure. A musician, maybe, or an actor or a scientist. Also, Marc wasn't Jewish, and that was no small thing in my family. Oh no, to become a member of the Solchik tribe, you had to show what you were made of. These were tough folks! People often think of Jews as people with their heads down, muttering over old books. But these were the calloused-hand Jews. These were the salt-of-the-earth Jews. They cared about culture and they cared about work. Did you know my uncle was the first Jewish tugboat captain of New York Harbor?"

I looked at her and shook my head.

"What, you think that's odd?"

I shook my head again, this time pityingly, and stood up to go. Her expression darkened.

"People like you, Nick, you mean well, but you're hand-icapped. You're ignorant. You think you know, but you don't. You don't know anything. You're Monarch, born and bred. What do you know, eh?"

"This is crazy," I said out loud, brusquely shrugging on my coat.

"I feel sorry for you," she said, "living your whole life like that. It was terrible of those people to do that to you. Of course *I* was involved as well."

"You know what?" I was now buttoning up my coat with a kind of brisk ferocity. "I've had just about enough of this, Mrs. Castor, and of these crazy strange hints you seem to be throwing out. I've come all this way out of politeness because you called me, and yet all you've done since I got here is mouth drunken gibberish."

"Are you getting angry with me, Nick?" She seemed delighted. "Please tell me you're getting angry with me. Are you going to cry now, big man?"

I was done.

"Your family has been very important to me over the years," I said, turning to go, "but I can promise you that I'll never expose myself to this kind of thing again. If you want to toy with someone, Mrs. Castor, get a dog. You need help, and it's not the kind of help that I can give. I really do hope you seek treatment, and soon. Good-bye." As I left I had a brief glimpse of her ruined, ancient face holding a kind of puckish joy.

"Tell your parents I saw you," I heard her say over my shoulder, "and that I wanted to tell you the truth, but decided not to. Tell them that. Tell them that for certain people, death is an upgrade, and I can't wait."

I heard the stab and drag of her footfalls receding into the house as I walked down the long main hall, opened the front door and let in the shock of living air and light.

# PART FOUR

# chapter 24

TWO HOURS AFTER THE TELEVISED PRESS conference announcing Rob's crime, local and state cop cars roared into the streets of Monarch with the speed of a beachfront landing. Men in creased pants and blocky white shirts and ties began strolling up and down the sidewalks, peering in the windows of shops, talking to intrigued, excited residents. The first of the news crews arrived—just a small van. And that feeling of strange and glary election began; that elevation into self-consciousness of the citizens of Monarch that would last for many weeks.

Within days, due to the massive local press coverage, there was a run on retired-area police detectives and investigators who could put an educated-sounding spin on the manhunt. One of the lucky ones was a man from a neighboring town named Gary Nathwire, who had just recently retired as a deputy county sheriff. Nathwire had the dramatic, authority-invoking widow's peak, the austere serious bone structure, and the drawling delivery that inspired confidence in viewers. He was married to a schoolteacher, had two kids and had lived and worked in the shadow of a notorious scandal-ridden sheriff's department for thirty years without ever being even minimally spattered by suspicion. Plus, he had a long history with fugitive cases. The producers fell on him with shouts of joy and we all quickly became familiar with his face.

From the beginning, Nathwire radiated a supreme confidence that Rob would quickly be apprehended. He explained just how difficult it is for someone, especially someone unskilled in the arts of evasion, to avoid a serious dragnet. Humans are sloppy creatures, he said. They deposit the cellular detritus of themselves on coffee cups in diners. They sticker everything they touch with their fingerprints. They leave "smell corridors" in the air easily traced by the highly developed olfactory neurons of bluetick hounds, and travel in hurricanes of paper and electronic transactions. Almost invariably, they plug into the traceable grid.

If none of that happens, Nathwire said, then often while drunk, at bars or in the midst of making sexual advances, they talk; they blab of their exploits; they draw heroic pictures of themselves under siege and outsmarting the long hand of the law.

Nathwire's granitic self-confidence never seemed to crack. He was absolutely certain that it would be only a matter of days until Rob was brought to justice.

And he was wrong.

A week after the press conference we were all still reeling; we were still sick at heart about the whole thing; we were still faintly thrilled, despite ourselves, by the advent of something quite this large, this lurid, this electric in our midst. And we were also, many of us I think, secretly rooting for Rob to continue to evade capture, though under the circumstances we would never have admitted it. I was driving to work that morning when I saw two state police cruisers parked in a kind of vector by the side of the road, their lights going. I pulled over not far away and sat in the car, watching. The decision to do so was immediate and unthinking.

The cops had a German shepherd with them, one of those animals that seem to contain a kind of pedigreed fury, erect, quivering, big pawed, alert through the tapered muzzle. The cops whispered something in the dog's ear, rubbed a piece of cloth under its nose, and it took off into the woods at a rollicking sprint. Sitting in my car, looking on quietly, I called the lab office on the cell phone and told them I'd be a little bit late.

The street we were parked on was a ways out of the downtown area, located in that district where the population density begins to open up to rolling, thickly forested hills. Called Cliffside for the way it skirts an old disused quarry, the road is not far from where I grew up. In the particular area where we were parked, a variety of trails cut away in several directions into the woods. I had the strangest inkling, as I sat there. I kept the inkling purposefully on the outer edges of my consciousness, but I felt it, distinctly.

After about ten minutes, the dog came streaking out of the woods. Whether dogs can smile is a question I've heard since I was a small child, but if a dog could, this one was sporting a killer grin. The dog was followed out of the woods about five minutes later by a plainclothes cop carrying something in a black plastic evidence bag. I got out of the car, and approached the cruiser.

Out here, this far from the big city, police and the law are courteous, laid back, and like neighbors, mostly, with the tiniest of authority-chips on their shoulders. They're a world away from *Homicide* and *NYPD Blue*.

"Morning, Officer," I said to the plainclothes cop, who nodded, silent at my greeting. "Any break in the case?"

"You media?" he asked.

"Not by a long shot." Smiling, I explained that I was just an old friend of Rob Castor, and that I was passing by. The cop took a long, measuring look at me, and then asked me my name. I told him, and he wrote it down on a small pad. Then he nodded to himself as if in confirmation that I'd passed some internal background check.

"Just a debris shelter," he said, motioning with his chin in an approximate direction in the woods. My heart jumped, but I said nothing, and nodded back soberly. "Could be a vagrant's, or it could be something more," he added.

"Huh," I said.

The man nodded, looked me over once again, and got slowly into the passenger side of his car. First his and then the other car, as if in a silent ballet, pulled out and left, one following the other. I stood there a long moment, listening, to make sure that they were out of sight, and then I got back in my own car. I sat there a few seconds while my hammering pulse slowed, before I pulled across the street, to an old construction site, and parked behind some brush. Then I got out of the car, squared my shoulders, and marched off into the woods.

I knew exactly where I was going. I cut through the woods along the trails I remembered more or less by heart, even twenty-odd years after the fact. It was high summer, and the green-leaf smell was strong. After about ten minutes, I made it to the brushy covert where Rob and I had first talked about breasts, and I had watched his foxy, sea green eyes open and close as he instructed me on the ways of the world. Dozens, maybe a hundred times total we'd gone there, and crushed the grass, and hung out in that essential enclosed space of childhood, auditioning our adult selves with each other. I stood there a long moment, remembering. Over the years, other people had found their way into our sanctuary, clearly, because there were crumpled cigarette packs, bits and pieces of old flaking food packaging, and even a rain-pulped paperback novel, its pages swollen in a rigid flower. Off to one side, I could see the blackened remnant of a campfire. Self-consciously, laughing inwardly to myself, I touched the darkened stones, but they were cold.

At a certain point I ambled across the clearing, wondering what it was they'd taken in an evidence bag. I was standing there, musing to myself, smiling slightly and totally lost in thought, when out of the sighing, wind-driven mix of forest sounds there came a strange call. Low and insistent, it came again.

I froze.

For about two years, when we were kids together, Rob had been big into birding. He'd carried field guides in a backpack, along with a pair of rubber-sheathed Leitz Trinovid binoculars, and often, a grubby life list rolled into his pocket. I enjoyed birds, but in the amateur way of someone simply relishing their designer good looks, though I did remember Rob's skill at mimicking their calls. I also remembered, years later, standing with him stoned one night in a park in Washington, D.C., deep in my unemployed pop-physics phase, and marveling at the shivering liquid notes of a particularly ambitious mockingbird.

The call came again, high, fluting on the air. It was a mournful sound, equidistant between a hoot and a bleat. It was coming from not that far away, somewhere in the woods on the other side of the clearing. I took a careful look around myself, and saw absolutely no one. For a long time I stood there, listening to the sound, the hair stirring on the back of my neck. Then I started slowly walking toward it.

# chapter 25

THE TEARS ARRIVED UNEXPECTEDLY, AT work. While filling out an order form for a wide-spectrum animal antibiotic manufactured by Knight Pharmaceuticals, I put down my pen and suddenly notified myself that I was about to start crying. It was the word "knight," which, given the rolling boil of my mind of late, had acted as a spur to memory, and flung my thoughts all the way back to a childhood recollection of playing chess with Marc Castor. I had often played chess with the calm, unflappable Marc Castor, and he'd nearly always beaten me—with this one exception. I had been down to my last few scattered pieces that day, and in a sudden flurry of moves I checkmated him and won. What I remembered was the shocked surprise on his face, and the way he'd turned around in his chair, as if to summon a doubting audience to witness this stunning reversal. From that day forward, I had carried within me the victory—and the look on his face—as part of the legend of my private expertise, and it was only now, sitting in my office, pen in hand, that I understood that Marc had let me win. It was a gift of his, a communication of a sort, and the sensation of reexperiencing it, akin to a living warm touch arriving at the end of a twenty-year-long arm, made me start to cry before I could stop myself.

It was clear what I had to do. I stood up from my desk, stalked out the back door into the parking lot (fully aware that my erratic recent behavior at work was increasingly becoming a subject of office conversation), drove straight to the travel agent, bought a ticket and then zoomed home to pack a bag.

When I got home, Lucy, alerted by my phone call, was waiting for me. I sat her down and told her that my father had had a "cardiac relapse" and that I had to fly out there immediately. I'm not sure why I didn't tell her the truth. Perhaps it's because, gradually and yet increasingly in the months since Rob Castor's death, the truth had become an enemy. She looked at me appraisingly as I embellished my falsehood, and then she reached forward and, to my surprise, gave me a sincere hug. As welcome as it was, the contact with her was also shocking—not least for the surge of sexual electricity that accompanied it. I hadn't had any physical contact with Lucy for several months, and I tried not to judge myself too harshly for the fact that, while her eyes communicated to me a moment of candid tenderness in which I could read, as in a series of fanned cards, her worry about my father, her grieving over our marriage, and her recent deep loneliness within it, my mind was blotted out with thoughts of the quivering pink and white sensitivities of her body.

When the hug was over and the strange, mixed circuit that had enclosed us for a second was broken, I turned to go. Almost certainly, by the time I was backing the car into the street, she was already on the phone to Purefoy.

On the way to the airport, I called my parents, to announce my imminent arrival. My mother was taut and defensive, as if she'd sensed something from the start, and she tried briefly to duck seeing me by mentioning something about her book club, but I barreled right over her. Shirley Castor had "explained everything," I said in a loud, clear voice, and I was coming down to "get some answers." Her stunned inhalation of breath told me everything I needed to know.

I showed up at their door feeling like a single large, projected bullet, shot from a gun two thousand miles away. Breathing deeply a moment, I rang.

My mother opened the door and pecked me on the cheek, her face giving away none of her inner feelings. "How was your flight?" she asked in a flat, tense voice. She had on a concealingly loose sky-blue shirt, a pair of dark blue shorts that made her legs look slightly bowed, and pointy sneakers. Her hair was perfectly set in its characteristic sexless bowl and flip, and I was sure she'd been to her salon that morning for a wash and style.

"Fine," I said, "and very smooth."

"That's good," she said, avoiding my eyes.

I smiled thinly, thinking, this is not a divorce, what we're doing now. A divorce happens in daylight, its facts are conscripted according to the fine print of contracts;

the children and properties are divided by law. But this is insidious, what was done to me. It's like being eaten by bacteria from the inside out.

"Nick," my father said from behind my mother. I went forward into the room, noting that he'd been upgraded from the infant uniform of pajamas to a pair of seersucker pants, a dress shirt and the requisite white sneakers. Strangely, he had his hat on, even though the back door to the patio was open, and through that door flowed the hot, thin desert air. My guess was that they'd opened it that morning and then received my call, and in the subsequent frenzy had simply forgot. Another time this would have provoked a reflex of sympathy on my part for the encroaching distractedness of age. But I was here, now, on different business. And it was clear that both my parents were girded for battle.

"Dad," I said, moving toward him, and then pulling myself up a few feet away—the impulse to embrace short-circuited.

"Okay," he said, as if acknowledging the newly chill climate between us. "Okay, then. So sit down."

My mother had scurried off into the kitchen, and returned as I was sitting down on the couch with a tray of chips, salsa and lemonade. She set it down in silence. My father was still grumblingly lowering himself onto the couch; the hinges of his knees invariably locked at a certain angle and he dropped through space the last few inches to the cushions in a silent free fall terrifying in its implications. "So, Nick," my mother said, "I'm so glad that all is going well with you"—she brought two hands up to her chest, and waved them around without obvious purpose—"in your job and everything at home with Lucy."

"Yeah." I took a long swallow of my lemonade and nodded.

"Okay," my father said, for the third time, "so here we are. One thing at a time. Strange as it seems, Nick, I'm glad you came."

"Are you," I said.

"I am, yes. You want some clarification, and we say fine to that. We owe you that, son"—and the word, so neutral in essence, seemed suddenly to flare a moment in the room—"at the very least. And we're going to give it to you."

"Everybody makes accommodations in life, and so did we," my mother said, in what was clearly a preemptive rhetorical strike. She sat down next to my father, her right hand fluttering to her lips. "It was a different time."

"So, let's talk," my father said.

"Fine," I said.

"You're wondering why it happened, of course," my father said.

"Yes, I am."

"You're thinking, possibly, 'Why would a man do this to a person he called his son.'"

"You could say that."

"A *very* different time, it was," said my mother.

"I wanna start with the big picture first," he said, "and one thing I'm gonna do as part of that is, I'm gonna level with you, okay?"

I nodded.

"You know depression, son? You know what it is?"

"I think I've got a vague idea."

"No, you don't, unless you've had it diagnosed. It's not being sad because you got dumped or passed over on the job or audited. It's like being trapped in some kind of smelly thick mud that closes over your head and you can't move or see or even get out of your own way. And me, okay, I admit it, I was depressed. Hey, I was even seeing a shrink," my father said astonishingly. "I was dejected about goddamn everything in the couple of years before your birth. And back then wasn't like today, you know, when it's like some new dance craze to be unhappy and everybody is doing it by the numbers, with the pills and the doctors. No, back then, you weren't only sad as hell, you were also embarrassed about it. Your mother would say, 'Larry, where are you? I can see you but you're not there.' Where was I? Good question! I'm not copping a plea here, I'm telling you I was suffering from not-wanting-to-be-alive disease. I was at the end of my rope, okay? So when what happened happened, and that despicable human person, that so-called friend of the family from across the street, who preyed on your lonely mom, calling her and dropping by constantly, drawing her in like a spider and wearing her down with his so-called compassion, because he could talk, yes he could—when he did that, and he took advantage of her good nature, well I guess what I'm saying is that it was just another bad thing happening among many. Also, it was like I was so far down inside myself that it was almost happening to someone else. Who knows, maybe it even made it a little easier to deal with, being depressed like that. And anyway, what do you think my choices were at that point, Nick?"

I simply stared at him.

"I'll tell you. They were two," he said in his high, weak voice. "They were either break up both of the families with a terrible fight of some kind, or fall on my sword and swallow it." After a pause, he said, "I swallowed it. You should be aware that it did not taste good. "

Above me, I could feel, rather than see, my mother twisting slowly from side to side, hands retracted to her chest in a posture of silent supplication. I took a deep drink from my glass, feeling anger at how the impalement of my life on the shaft of convenience was about to be subsumed into yet another story in my parents' anthology of "what we had to do to survive."

"Why didn't you just abort me, Mom?" I asked.

"Oh, for Christ's sake!" said my father.

"Nick"—her voice was soft to the point of nearly inaudible—"please, why would you ask me such a thing?"

She reached out to touch my brow, but I jerked my head away from her. "Don't do that, Nick. Please don't do that. I didn't want an abortion because I wanted *you*. I wanted exactly what I got, which was a wonderful person in my life. I wanted you. I got you. I'm incredibly proud of you. That's why."

"The doctor said she had a thin-walled uterus," my father said, frowning, "and the abortion would have been very dangerous. Besides, she's right, we wanted the child. We didn't want Patrick to grow up without siblings."

"We made accommodations," my mother said.

"We came to a kind of agreement," he added.

"It was a different time," she said.

I shut my eyes and felt how on the far side of anger ran the deep, nearly bottomless canyons of inner fatigue.

How tired I was just then! I could have gone instantly to sleep right on the sofa.

"An agreement about my future without my participation," I said, opening my eyes, "is not much of an agreement, from where I'm standing."

There was a silence, during which my father looked down at the ground, and my mother, unable to stay still, took a swift couple of forward steps, but immediately converted the movement into aimlessly adjusting some photographs on a nearby tea table.

"Pardon me, guys, but I still can't get my head around this." I laughed hollowly. "I mean, when would you have told me if I hadn't come to you now?"

"That was probably the worst part of the whole thing," my mother said quickly, looking up from the photographs, "that we'd started this train in motion, and then you were already a grown man with your own family, and we still couldn't stop the train. We didn't know how to stop it. We wanted to, but it all seemed too late, and we were afraid that it would only create, what, bitterness and difficulty."

"Regrettable," my father said, "it was regrettable, yes."

"Regrettable?" I asked, and laughed again, this time with a high, braying sound, feeling yet another wall of self-control come down with a slam. "A day of rain is regrettable, guys. Failing a test is regrettable. Missing a doctor's appointment is regrettable. But having lived your entire life as a fucking lie is one whole hell of a lot more than just 'regrettable.'"

But my father merely replied calmly, "There was no lie involved."

"What are you talking about?"

"Of omission, maybe, Nick," he said. "But we didn't think of it like that. We thought of it as what we needed to do to save our own family, and give you the best life possible. And look at you now," my father said, "all your arms and legs, a nice wife, a good career, two sons and a—"

"Stop it!" I shouted.

My father looked to my mother and shrugged his shoulders. Then he turned back to me and shook his head, as if in regret. "Stop what, Nick?" he asked.

"Just please stop this horseshit charade, Dad. Stop trying to pretend that everything was always normal and hunky-dory save for some small little out-of-the-way details." I got to my feet, my hands involuntarily making sharp chopping motions in the air. "Don't think everything's fine. Everything's not fine. I'm having an affair, I'm probably going to get a divorce, and I've taken so much time off from my job lately I may be out of work soon too. My life is falling apart, okay?" I saw my mother recoil. "Are you happy now, Mom? Is this the bastard child you were so fucking proud to raise?"

"Is such language really necessary?" said my mother.

"*Language?*" I grabbed either side of my head. "Can you stop caring for one goddamn minute about language and what is proper and nice? Can you just stop," I was shouting, "for one whole minute pretending that we're all trying out for the perfect goddamn family!"

"Go ahead," said my father, lying back amid the cushions, "yell, scream, blow off some steam, son. It'll make you feel better. You're entitled."

"What in God's name did you think you were doing?" I cried.

"Love doesn't need excuses." My mother was talking faster now; she'd probably gone over this for years with her own battery of therapists and was down to her prepared lines. "We brought love into being, that's the important thing. We loved you very much and you wanted for nothing. Every life has rain falling in it; there are bad days and skeletons in every single closet in the world. People die early, they go crazy, their marriages blow up. But on balance we gave you everything we could."

"Except the truth," I said, and then turned to my father. "And as for you, should I call you Dad, or Larry? Should I call you a sad sack stand-in who never had the balls to tell me the truth, or something else? Dad?"

There was a silence.

"Whew," my father said, turning to my mother. "He's really going after me today, isn't he? I can't say as I like it, and I can't say as I'm going to take it. You wanna apologize, son?"

"No."

"No?"

"No," I said.

My father nodded, as if he expected this. With an effort, he struggled to his feet, and began walking into the bedroom. I saw his frailness, his unsteadiness on his feet, and it took an effort of will to keep up my rage. But I managed, feeding it the pieces of his lie and of the loss in my life I'd never be able to make up. He paused at the entrance to the room and said, "You're turning this nasty, which must be what you wanted to do. Well, what I want you to know, before I tell you to go to hell forever—"

"Larry," my mother said.

He raised his hand like a traffic cop, palm up. "What I want you to know is that first of all, people who live in glass houses, you get me? If you're having an affair, that's fine and your business. But if out of that affair you have a child, then what? As for myself, I was out of the loop here. I was the injured party. Do you think I was happy with the situation, you little shit?"

I heard my mother gasp. In all our life, growing up, "off-color" words had never been spoken.

"I did my best to love you as my own child and I tried always to think of you that way, as my own flesh and blood. I used to talk about you, did you know that? Yeah, I used to brag about you. Those papers you published in college in the *Biological Review*—I don't think there was an ear in Monarch I didn't bend. You forget, because you've got this chip on your shoulder, that I walked you through life. Maybe I was shut down on some levels, but you never wanted for anything. What parents do—does it add up to anything in the book of life? Who knows. But you see only one side of things, Nick. I understand you're grieving now. It was terrible what happened to you—maybe, but on the other hand, maybe not. And I've got my grief too. I'm old and heading out into the dark. I could be bitter about it, I could resent and blame, but what's the point, and why should I? I'm what I made of myself, not what a bunch of other people thought about me. The blame game is a waste of time. If you can make your peace with that, fine. If not, well, have fun fighting." Entering the bedroom, he slowly shut the door.

I let out the breath I'd been holding and sat back on the couch. Distantly, like hearing Shakespeare from the back row, I was aware that he'd given a noble speech full of noble thoughts, but mainly what I was just then was disappointed. I was disappointed because what I was craving more than anything else at that moment was to be able to slam a burning spear into his side. Somehow, although I knew my mother was as fully or even more to blame, it was *him* I wanted revenge against first; *him* I wanted to impale painfully upon the truth before I got around to her. I knew this made no sense, but it didn't matter. I'd wanted him to be able to mark this day as the blackest, direst day he'd ever known, and instead, I felt somehow denied by him all over again.

Left alone in the room with me, my mother was hanging her head.

"I feel like a middle-aged man witnessing his first primal scene," I said, and laughed mirthlessly. "I feel almost perfectly empty, in fact."

"I understand," she said. And then, after a moment, tentatively, she asked, "Do you mind if I say something?"

"No."

"I'm not sure anything happens finally for a reason, Nick, despite what religion says. Sometimes things simply happen and that's that. Your brother," she said in an unnaturally hushed, silent voice, "was a difficult baby, and I was alone in the big new house and your father was elsewhere, for what seemed like months on end. Men do that occasionally, especially when their firstborn children are sons, I think. They kind of go away and watch from afar, maybe out of jealousy a little bit, and other things as well. And then I was so tired, tired like eating sand, tired like forgetting I'd ever had energy and ever would again."

She stopped, thoughtful, waiting for me to say something. When I didn't, she went on, "But what I want you to know is this, Nick. I loved your father. I loved him then, after what happened, and I love him now. People do foolish rash things, like I did, without stopping loving. It's the human heart, that strange thing." She smiled sadly, knit her hands together and unknit them again. "And I can tell you something else as well, which is that finally, after you were born, when the worst of your father's anger began to lessen, and he could talk to me again, and he told me he still loved me, well, I don't think I've ever loved a person more in my life. Sacrifice," she said, "is very beautiful in a man. Some of the noblest things in life come as the result of sacrifice."

She was expecting me to speak, and I raised my head and looked at her from the far side of all I'd learned in the last few weeks. For a long moment, I struggled to find the warm undisturbed deeps of the heart where compassion lived. But compassion at that moment eluded me. I thought suddenly of Rob Castor, and a bitter, strangely copper taste rose in my mouth, and the blood beat hard in my head while I looked at the woman who had brought me into this world and I told her the truth. "You disgust me," I said, getting up to go.

# chapter 26

WHAT WAS HAPPENING TO ME? IT WAS AS if the violent subtraction of Rob from life had produced a wind of sorts, a strong cross draft that had blown away the fake stage set of my paternity, and in doing so, helped speed the ruin of my marriage, estranged me from my children, sent my father into the hospital and, most recently, driven a stake through the heart of my relationship with the only biological parent I had left. If his death hadn't actually caused these things, it had somehow crucially been a party to them. At bottom, added to the vulnerability of all that sheer exposure, was bewilderment. How was it that the demise of one person could have started such a spiraling, near-fatal injury cascade in another's life?

In the days after I returned from seeing my parents, I often had the sense of fissioning into two people, one of whom, corrected by the harsh truth, could watch the other still enacting the dream of his own biological continuity.

I knew that I'd constructed an entire personality around my supposed father's vocation of industrial chemistry. His worn books on the shelf with their endless replicating carbon-molecule diagrams had sent me floundering along the track of science and the march of deductive reason in life; his seeming inability to talk with me about any of the things I'd held most dear had produced in me an expertise in certain muted interrogatory conversational styles, the better to cross this breach, while driving me steadily toward my mother and producing in me a nearly feline awareness of other people's thoughts. These things were the essential, originary facts of my life. They were already in the bank. They'd happened. They could not be undone. But what did it mean that they were false? Leaving aside the sickness I felt at heart, what did it mean? And what did it mean that my real father, week after week, year after year, had stared at me living my life literally fifty feet from his front door until the day of his death, and never once, for my sake, let the mask slip from his face?

Under the circumstances, it was clear that there was only one person in the world I could talk to about this. Belinda and I had had little contact after our initial liaison beyond the few scattered affectionate e-mails, because both of us, I think, had reacted to the event by retracting back, in the manner of adulterers eager to conceal our crime. Though I'd been shocked and intermittently repentant about what I'd done, I was also aware that I was capable of repeating it. The icky knowledge that she was officially my half sister gummed up that desire, even if it did not entirely extinguish it. But I called her anyway. Heartfelt conversation with Lucy was impossible right now, and as regards other close friends, my life (like that of most men) has in part been a slow, steady shedding of the confidantes and close acquaintances of youth.

"I know everything," Belinda said as I entered her hotel room. She was wearing jeans and a tight T-shirt embla-zoned with the word "Killbilly," and she was holding her hands over her ears, and shaking her head with her mouth in a perfect ridged O of shock. "My mom told me this morning when I went over with Hiram to stage the inter-vention," she said. "Oh, God"—reaching out to hug me— "but is this too wild for words or what?"

Rather than talk, for a moment, I simply held her in my arms, relishing the sturdiness of her, the warmth, and beneath that warmth, the familiar budding live energy of the front of her body.

"Belinda," I said finally, letting go of her.

"How are you, Nick?"

"How am I?" I made a face. "Basically, numb. I feel like I'm on a reality television show and I stepped through a door and woke up in someone else's life."

"Well, in a certain sense, that's exactly what happened. Come over and sit down, honey, you look bushed."

Smiling, she beckoned me to the couch, and held my hand as we sat down together. Then she leaned forward, and stared at me a moment, big eyed, blinking.

"Brother?" she asked.

"Sister?" I responded.

"Can you believe this shit?"

"Barely," I said.

"Actually, I'm trying to think," she said, "if there's an opportunity here somehow."

"For what?"

She smiled at me from far away. "Growth."

"I'm not sure I compute."

"In the words of my roshi, 'Every treasure is guarded by dragons.' The fabric of your world got ripped open, Nick. Maybe you now have the chance to go through that opening and find your truth."

"I appreciate the beautiful sentiment," I said, frowning, "but practically speaking, what do I do once I find this truth? How do I process it? Are there fake-dad classes? Are there lessons you can take in how not to hate the people who brought you up in a lie?"

"Nick," she said gently, shaking her head. "Come on."

"No, really. I mean it. I already know I'm going to spend the rest of my life trying to find out why this happened and who this man named Marc Castor was at bottom. I mean, who was he really? I know he was basically a nice guy who smelled of dry-cleaning fluid and had a year-round tan, but what motivated him to do what he did? He couldn't have been the simple person he seemed, because simple guys don't bang the lady across the street and never tell their own bastard kids the truth, do they?"

Saying nothing, Belinda lit a cigarette.

"The hardest thing of all," I said, "is the knowledge that he's not coming back, ever, and that there's this whole world that brought me into being, and of about a million conversations to do with me and my future that I'll never know. At the center of it all is our father." There was a pause. "Our father," I repeated the word, tasting it. Before I knew it, I was adding harshly, "That piece of shit!"

Belinda watched me, saying nothing.

"That unbelievable asshole piece of shit," I said, trying it out.

She nodded, as if in agreement. Then she said, "Go on."

"Fucking jerk."

"More."

"Goddamned weakling. Unbelievable shitbag coward. Total spineless fuck."

There was another silence.

"I could cry," I said.

She continued to study me calmly.

"Maybe you should cry, Nick. Maybe that's exactly what you should do."

"Will you help me?" I asked.

"Help you?"

"Tell me something to make it happen?"

"To cry?"

"Yes. Tell me something I don't know? I'm gonna spend the rest of my life filling in blanks. Tell me something solid I can hold on to and get fucked up over, please."

She furrowed her brow. "Why?" she asked.

"Because I need it. Tell me"—the words appeared in my mouth without me thinking—"about his death."

"What?"

"Tell me how he died," I said, relishing the finality of the words, "tell me about it. It's the last time he was in the world. I wanna know about it. Tell me, Belly."

She took a long, thoughtful inhale on her cigarette. "You want," she said, as if to reassure herself she'd heard right, "that I tell you about his death."

"Yes," I said.

"His death, right."

"Please."

"Okay." She shook her head, composed herself a second before she spoke. "Well, his death was like most . . . deaths, actually. One day he was there, and the next he wasn't."

"How did he go?" I asked.

"I guess the best answer is gently. It was like smoke drifting out the window."

"Uh-huh."

"Actually"—I watched her eyes narrow slightly as she concentrated, remembering—"I'm convinced he wanted to leave, at the end. The cancer had hollowed him out like a seashell, and he couldn't do much. On top of that, the pain meds had destroyed his memory, and so he just lay there, while we played house around his bed. It was this big theater piece in which we pretended that he was just a little bit indisposed and would get better soon, even though we all knew he wouldn't, including him."

I grabbed her hand, squeezed it. "Good," I said, "this is beginning to hurt. I like it."

She rolled her eyes, cigarette in her mouth. "My mother was the main actor in the thing. She was such a self-involved bitch that it kind of surprised me what a trouper she became when the chips were down. She spent what seemed like weeks camped out next to him in bed, reciting her lines, which were that everything was going to be okay, and that they were going to try it all over again, the two of them, and this time, they'd get it right. I'd never felt they liked each other all that much, but you wouldn't have known it from the way she was behaving toward the end. He couldn't eat or sleep much by then, and she curled him up on her lap and sang him this crazy song about how young and beautiful he was, and how he was sweeping her off her feet, and he listened and smiled and even seemed to enjoy it. It was his good-bye kiss, his last generosity. That basic kindness of his—I'm not sure what good it ever did anybody, but it makes him a hell of a man in my eyes."

She stubbed out her cigarette.

"Better," I said. "It's killing me. Keep going."

"Nick," she said.

"Make me cry!" I was suddenly adamant. "Just do it!"

She muttered something indistinct to herself, and then raised her eyes and looked at me, nearly challengingly. "The last thing he said to me was that he would always love me," she said in a strong, clear voice, "and that he'd known, even when I pretended to hate him when I was a teenager, that I didn't, and that I was just being a kid. That was when I started crying, even though we'd all agreed none of us would in front of him. He smiled then, like he knew I'd just busted up our agreement, and I grabbed his hand and held it. We sat there for a while, saying nothing, while I listened to his breathing, which was thick and slow. The hospice worker who was there must have alerted everyone, because then the room silently filled up with the rest of us. I think he was relieved actually, I think he was happy the last part was beginning. Very slowly, his breathing got deeper and raspier, his eyes closed, and someone held his forehead, and each of us held one of his hands. They were beautiful hands, and you could tell they'd belonged to someone who knew how to do things in life. I sat there as the hands gradually unclenched. I don't know how much time went by. The morphine was hitting pretty hard, and I held his wrist while the pulse grew slower and slower. It was like his heart was climbing a staircase right out of his body. There had to be a last pulse, and there was. There was a pulse where his spirit took leave of his body. I imagined it as flinging a leg out forward over the void, and then stepping away forever. His face was utterly calm. Good-bye, I said. There was a chorus of whispered good-byes from around me. Good-bye. Good-bye. I kissed him on the forehead. Someone pulled me away from him. I don't remember much after that."

"Thank you," I said stiffly. And then, furiously, I was crying at last. "Thank you very much."

# chapter 27

THE VERY NEXT DAY, I DID SOMETHING I'D never done before. I went out and bought new clothes. It was a snap decision, made without the least hesitation. I drove over on my lunch hour to a local clothing store popular with college kids, where I purchased jeans, a pair of black form-fitting T-shirts and some European boots with thick soles and heels. I knew the T-shirts would be less than flattering on my untoned body, but I didn't care. The word *shitkicker*, applied by the clerk to my choice of boots, stuck in my head.

Never in my life have I been especially conscious of how I dressed. Lucy has always bought my clothes, and my wardrobe, in the main, is two toned, with the default color options running toward brown and dark green. My footwear tends toward the comfortably crepe soled. My shirts are typically loose, button-down affairs, purchased at the local Daffy's, or bought at the Marshalls discount store at the mall in Utica.

I didn't wear these new clothes to either the office or home. I merely kept them in my desk drawer at work, the whole bunch of them, and took them out from time to time, and smelled the fresh sizing of the fabric and the leather of the shoes, and felt myself comforted by this in a way I couldn't explain. The clothes seemed somehow to provide me with a lifeline of sorts, an implied way through the storm ahead.

I needed the way. The storm was thickening fast. Lucy was now seeing Purefoy often, and I knew—because I'd begun checking her e-mail—that she had decided to spend some of her small hoarded inheritance on a four-day "Sacred Intimacy Retreat" in a local mountain monastery, where Purefoy had an advisory role of some sort. Lucy had never been particularly New Agey. If anything, both of us were invested in a hard, rational view of life. The fact that she was undertaking such a thing, with a "master of the Tantric sexual universe" named Thomas Wing, and paying two thousand dollars for the privilege of discovering things like "how to use the body as a vehicle of ecstatic dissolution" was a deep surprise.

Alone in my office, I first tried to laugh harshly at the idea. But the laughter slowed when I checked out Thomas Wing on the Internet and beheld a photo of a muscular, square-jawed man looking at me with the kind of fore-knowledge of my own foibles that seemed perilously close to desire for my wife. I immediately clicked off the Web site, leaned back in my squeaking desk chair, shut my eyes, and though I knew it was absolutely useless at this late date, dictated to the world an emotional letter imploring the happy-sad god of marriage to help us rekindle the

flame of our feeling, Lucy and I, and in the process, redis-
cover our loyalty not only to each other, but to the original
sunrise picture of marriage and children under whose sway
we'd first fallen in love.

Fear is a wonderful motivator. Momentarily refreshed
by this inner operation, I went home and enjoyed the
queer luxury of being surprised, as if for the first time,
by the deep domestic coldness I'd been so instrumental in
bringing to life.

At work the next day, I dressed carefully in my new
clothes. Spending at least twenty minutes or so in front
of the mirror in my office, I savored the strange visual
impression of myself, balding and plump, swelling a pair
of pencil-leg jeans and a black T-shirt. Then, wearing the
boots that, due to their chunky heels, altered my sight line
by a perceptible half inch and gave me the vaguely privi-
leged feeling of looking down on myself, I walked out the
office door, leaving, I noticed, a trail of frozen conversations in my wake.

I was bound for lunch with Mac. A couple of days earlier he had phoned and amid his usual hurricane of blus-
tery insincerities had asked to see me because he needed
some more "texture" for his book from the "way-back
time when we were all kids together." Only someone, he'd
said, "who'd played in the Castor sandbox" could give
him what he needed. Feeling flattered to be included, and
overriding my own inherent suspicions about the man, I'd
said yes.

Swiftly I now crossed the main street of town. I was
headed for Star's Diner. I had insisted on meeting Mac
there. It was the smaller, more out of the way of the town's

two eateries, and the place where, aside from a particularly hammy pea soup, there was less chance of being bullied into fake-amiable conversation with remote acquaintances.

"Dag," Mac cried from his booth as I swung through the front door of the restaurant. "If it ain't Mr. Hiply Swinging Dude!"

While heads swiveled around, I made a tunnel with my eyesight and walked stiffly into it.

"Hey, people change," I said, sliding into the booth across from him with my cheeks burning.

"Well, I guess so." He rose and extended his hand, and I noticed his face creased by strange retention lines as he struggled not to laugh. "Wow." He sat back down again, looking me up and down. "You look great, actually."

"Do I?"

"Hell, yeah."

I said nothing for a moment, and watched as he forced a smile onto his face, leaned forward, and asked in his most resonantly guy-chummy voice, "So how are you, pal?"

"I'm all right," I said quietly, "the usual strange—" But then I stopped myself, because really, what could I say? It's never been so weird? My whole existence has been based on false pretences? I've been putting it sexually to my half sister, and by the way, I'd like to arrest Lawrence Framingham on suspicion of impersonating—badly—a dad?

"Actually, life is fine, thanks," I said.

"That's good."

"Yeah. And you?"

"Not bad," he said, "but as I told you over the horn, I'm kind of feeling the pinch." He mock-throttled himself.

"What about?" I asked.

"Time, in a word. Fucking editor's breathing down my throat. Wants an excerpt for something called the 'Book Expo.'" He pronounced the last two words as if they tasted bad.

"Huh." I had no idea what he was talking about.

"I keep hearing that little tweedle-dee voice of his in my head, 'It's time sensitive, you gotta slam it out.' I told him, cool your jets, Tex. I'm an artist." Mac pronounced that word with grandiloquent pride. "And I ain't gonna be rushed."

He laughed invitingly, extra loud, his small eyes on mine while his hand crawled casually to the center of the table and switched on a tiny tape recorder.

"What's that?"

"Just a little backup," he said, "in case I get so blown away by what you have to say that I forget to write it down."

"Funny."

"Standard procedure, really."

I said nothing for a moment.

"If it makes you uncomfortable . . . ," he said.

"Actually, it does."

He reached forward again and switched it off.

"No prob."

He surveyed the menu a moment in silence, and then raised his eyes. "So, you been much in touch with the Castor family lately?"

"No, not especially," I said.

"Me neither. And Belinda?"

"What about her?" I watched his eyes, filled with a crafty light, ticking back and forth across my face.

"I just remembered," he said, "that you two were an item many moons ago."

"We've gotten together recently," I said.

He stared at me. "And how is the world's oldest Janis Joplin impersonator these days?"

"Actually, she's pretty messed up."

"Too bad, but who can blame her. The two of them were incredibly tight, weren't they?"

"Like peas in a pod," I said.

"Frigging Rob," Mac said, apropos of nothing.

"I know," I said, feeling, again, the relief I always felt when I was able to talk about him to someone. "It's weird, but I think I feel closer to him now in some way, all these months after his death, than I did the last time I saw him."

"When was that, by the way?" he asked smoothly.

"What?"

"The last time you saw him."

I looked at him, puzzled. "At New Russian Hall, of course," I said. "Weren't you there?"

"*Was* that the last time you saw him alive?"

"What are you getting at?"

"Do you really want to know?"

"Wait a minute, you *were* there, Mac, I remember now. Of course you were."

"Yes, I was. In fact, I remember the evening quite well." He was giving me the stare again.

"What?"

"Nothing."

The waitress arrived and we placed our orders.

"I'd like to ask you again," he said when she had left.

"Please do."

"*Was* that in fact the last time you saw him alive?"

I placed my hands on the table, interlaced my fingers.

"What the hell are you getting at, Mac?" I asked.

He let his gaze wander desultorily around the restaurant as if he were barely paying attention, and then looked directly into my face.

"Nick," he said, "you should know that I've got friends at the cop shop."

"So?" I said, suddenly feeling a cramping sensation in the pit of my stomach, as if something, a fold of muscle, was grabbing for traction.

"So I know stuff, Nick."

"Well, isn't that nice for you."

"I know stuff," he repeated, "about what happened that day."

"Which day?"

"The last day you saw Rob alive."

"Do you."

"Yes, I do." As if in the grip of immense sadness, he sighed. "I've got a report from a state trooper who placed you in a spot about six days after the murder, out by Cliffside Road, where, if memory serves, you and Rob used to meet."

"I see."

"Look, Nick, scout's honor that if you have something you want to tell me it's utterly off the record, unless you want it included. I wouldn't do anything that could possibly lead to a charge of suppressing evidence at the trial."

"Ah, a threat now? Lovely. Besides, earth to Mac: the trial already happened."

"It's not a threat, it's a simple fact. As to the trial, well,

word is that her sad-sack parents are gonna give it one
more college try and sue Simkowitz, the owner of their
old building on the Upper West Side."

"No!"

"Yeah, on a charge of negligence, because the front-
door lock was broken."

"Unbelievable, another trial, God," I said, and found
myself, despite the charged moment, again recalling the
gray sandstone "Justice Center," along with the yammer-
ing of the bulge-eyed lawyers, the endless stream of witnesses, and the thin, conservatively dressed sixty-something
couple who were Kate's parents, flown in from Ohio. The
father had the deaconish face of a church elder, and the
mother was a starved-looking woman whose prettiness,
sliding fast toward the crumpled and sexless, was recalled
only by an extravagant flounce of graying curls.

"To this day," I said, in an effort to change the subject,
"I've never understood why they sued. I mean, their daughter was gone, and they had enough money for the rest of
their lives already. What good would it be to have another
half million, and go through that grisly fucking coroner's
report, for example?"

"It's an interesting question. I think they were actually
vengeful," Mac said.

"How so?"

"I think they were so blind and crazy with grief that
they kind of defaulted into rage and tried to make the system hurt somebody as a way to feel better. Many people
do." Mac paused a second. "But let's talk about you."

For some reason, the memory of the trial and Kate's
American Gothic parents must have brought a faint smile

to my face, because he now added, "You're finding this funny."

"No I'm not."

"Yes you are. I'm sitting here right across from you and you're finding it funny. Is it really that funny?"

"Give it a rest, Mac."

"Don't make me beg." He reached over and switched on the recorder. While staring at the glow of the tiny red light, I heard him say, "I'm asking you, plain and simple, man-to-man and friend-to-friend, to take me back to that day, that afternoon when you saw the cop on Cliffside Road. What'd you do next? Quick, before you can think about it!"

At that moment, I remembered something Rob had said a couple years earlier, when we'd run into each other by surprise at a party in Monarch. He'd been drunk, and launched on one of his great conversational spirals, and he'd been talking about the way in which ancient cultures had tried to resist their own disappearance by sending proofs of their existence forward into future time. He'd said their measures had ranged from sheer mass, as in the pyramids, to sheer withdrawal, as in the Lascaux caves. But it didn't matter what they did, he added, because time was a pig and would eventually root all their secrets open to the light. That being the case, he said, leaning forward and winking at me, it paid to be honest, because everyone was gonna find out everything anyway.

"Maybe I know something," I said. "But even if I do, why should I tell you?"

Mac nodded, as if expecting this. He tilted his head slightly, and made a wave of softness go over his features.

"Nick," he said quietly, "we go way back, don't we."

"Yes, we do."

"Does it mean something, do you think?"

"What?"

"That we're basically the only two people not in his family who knew Rob from the beginning?"

"I don't know."

"Well, I'll tell you something, it does. It means something to Rob and it means something to you and me."

"You and me?" I asked, dubious.

He shrugged and then opened his arms wide. "Hey, I'm not your enemy, you know. I'm just a buddy from the way back who wants to do right by you and our dear departed pal as well."

"Uh-huh," I asked, "and would a bestselling book happen to factor into what you want?"

"You know"—he ignored me—"for the longest time I've been wanting to have you over, see you more. But everything's been so crazy lately that I haven't gotten around to it."

"When, like over the last ten years?"

"Now you're simply being unkind. Hey"—he smiled— "remember that time we all had lunch together and you and Janine had such a laughing fit that I thought you'd bust a gut?"

Janine was his wife.

"Yes," I said, "and I also remember that the only reason I was there was because I was accompanying Rob."

"The point"—he shut his eyes in irritation while continuing to smile—"is that I miss seeing you more often, Nick. We should hang out together, rekindle the old flame."

"A touching thought," I said.

Mac opened one eye, and looked at me. "Okay," he said, "you think I'm full of shit, and you probably have your reasons."

"Thank you."

"But that doesn't change the fact that you know something I need, and I'm gonna get it out of you one way or another, my friend."

"Ah," I said, "that's better. Welcome back."

"Ha." Mac laughed out loud, as did I. And then, sitting there chuckling, I had the sudden thought that maybe I should reach out, if that's the right word, and take the opportunity offered me to start draining the swamp of evasions in which I'd been paddling in circles for what felt like months. Maybe I should begin owning up. But what did it mean that the agent of my candor would be none other than the professionally slippery Mac Sterling? Then again, at this late date, what other options did I have?

"I'll give you five minutes," I said.

Mac shut his eyes for a brief moment, as if to savor his happiness, and then said softly, "Oh good."

"But you're a shit for ambushing me this way."

He put his fist to his heart.

"Forgive me."

"Doubtful," I said.

He did his best to look abashed.

"Okay, let's see," I said, still frowning, "I'll begin at the beginning. I did in fact meet the cops, as it turns out. You were right about that. I was just driving by, and I saw them parked on the side of the road, and I pulled off myself and asked them what was going on. They said they'd found an old debris shelter, and had some stuff in an evidence bag they took away."

As if afraid to derail my train of thought, Mac stared frozenly down at the table.

"After they drove off," I said, "I sat there awhile in my car, and then I parked it out of sight across the road, and decided to investigate my hunch. I walked into the woods and followed an old trail I knew, a shortcut. The trail eventually led to the place where they'd just come from gathering evidence, the cops."

"The covert," he said. And then when he saw me recoil, he raised both his hands, and said, "Sorry, you talk, I'll listen."

"It wasn't the covert," I said, "but it was a clearing near the covert. Were you ever there?"

"Maybe once," he said, and then, after a pause, "go on."

"Well, I walked into that clearing, and obviously I was a little what, half freaked out, because I had this feeling, of course, that maybe something was going on. And then I heard it."

"What?"

"The sound."

"What sound?"

"A bird call," I said, "that I recognized from long ago."

Mac picked up his pen, his mouth falling open.

"No shit!"

"Yup. I remember I stood there a long time, trying to place that call. It seemed like it was kind of shifting in the wind a little bit, like it was coming from one place, and then another."

"Rob had been a bird-watcher, hadn't he?"

"Big time," I said. "I even remember overhearing him trying to pick up a girl at a party by telling her he was 'into the macho side of bird-watching,' whatever that means."

Carefully, holding my eye while doing so, Mac laughed.

"And then?" he asked, in a low voice.

"Then what?"

"Then what happened?"

"Then I followed the sound for a bit. But I was unsure, at first. There was a lot of wind noise, as I say, which made the whole thing a bit confusing. But finally, it seemed to me that it was coming from the original old covert."

"Damn!"

"I know. I was pretty freaked by then, because I had a feeling that something real was definitely about to happen."

The waitress approached the table with a pot of coffee, but Mac, before she could even speak, waved her away with a crisp big-city flick of the fingers. She stalked off in a huff.

"That wasn't nice," I said.

"I know," he said impatiently. "And then?"

"Then the call came again, and it was definitely coming from the covert, I was sure of it. It had been many years since I'd been there, of course. Maybe ten or twenty, who knows. My heart was beating so hard as I neared it that I'm not even sure I could hear anymore."

"I'm about to have a heart attack just listening to this," said Mac.

"It was clear," I went on, "that other people had discovered the hideout, because I could see some trash at the entrance to it."

"Trash?"

"Yeah, old books, some rubbers, tin cans. Stuff like that."

"Okay."

"And I was freaking out now. My heart was really whamming in my chest, and I felt like maybe I was in the *Blair Witch Project* or something. But I forced myself to move forward, step by step. Then I reached the little opening to the covert. The call came again. I was certain I knew the call. I took a deep breath, and I ducked under the opening and then crouched in the dimness, while my eyes adjusted."

I paused while Mac, placing both hands on the table, rose involuntarily a few inches upward from his seat.

"Then what?" he said in a breathless voice.

"Then I saw it, Mac."

"What?"

"It."

"What, it?" he whispered.

"This kind of huge-looking bluebirdy thing called a Steller's jay. It looked at me like it knew something, and it made the call again, like someone gargling with marbles."

"A what, a bird?" Mac said, slowly sitting down, uncomprehending. "What do you mean, a bird?"

"I know, I was flipping out. It seemed utterly impossible that a bird was sitting in the middle of this covert, in this enclosed space, and that it wasn't afraid of me either. I have to tell you, Mac, it was pretty damn weird!"

"A bird?" I watched his face fall down a series of disappointed stairs. "Not a bird!"

"Yeah, what a letdown, right? Think how I felt."

He looked at me, shook his head with a harsh, bitter

little laugh, leaned forward as if to say something nasty, and then pulled himself back again and retracted his hands to his chest like a poker player protecting his draw from prying eyes.

"A bird," he repeated for about the fourth time, "you're telling me a bird."

"I'm telling you a bird."

"That's your story."

"Yup."

"Right." And with that, abandoning any pretense of friendship, he stood up, grabbed his tape recorder, snapped his notebook closed, and, leaning down close, in a voice loud enough for the entire restaurant to hear, shouted, "Well fuck you to hell!"

Then he walk-jogged out the front door.

# chapter 28

HEART BEATING HARD, I LET MY EYES adjust to the dimness and saw him sitting across from me, leaning back against a stump, and grinning. The impact was as violent as a physical blow, yet I also felt somehow that I'd been waiting for this moment for several days—or maybe, come to think of it, a long time.

"Hey," he said, calmly.

A sound came out of my chest—something thick and unfledged—and then I lunged toward him, and a moment later we were slamming into each other and hugging furiously.

"Rob!" I cried into his neck. We leaned back and held each other's elbows. "Unbelievable!"

"So how ya doing?" he asked.

"I just knew it!" I yelled.

He was skinnier than I'd ever seen him, skinnier even than he'd been a week before at New Russian Hall, and his face, below the disorderly blond beard, was raw, reddish, and full of strange bumps and welts. Silently he put a long finger to his lips.

"The trees have ears," he whispered. "Keep it down."

"I can't believe this!" I cried softly. "Rob, what's going on? I mean," I stumbled, "what's going on!"

He scratched his chin energetically and smiled his canny old smile. "Well," he said, "let's see. I'm out in our childhood cave with one of my best hometown friends just now. And it's a lovely summer day too. How's by you?"

I laughed. "Where have you—you know I can't quite get my mind around—what the hell are you doing here?"

"What does it look like I'm doing?"

"You know that the whole world is looking for you, right?"

"So I understand."

There was a beat of silence. The sun, interrupted by leaves, striped us with wicker-colored light. Birdsong bubbled in the trees around us.

"What's up?" he asked.

"What's up?" I laughed explosively for a moment, and then abruptly stopped. I shook my head. "I guess my first question," I said, "is what the hell are we doing here at all? How did this happen?"

"Beats me," he said calmly. "I guess the answer depends on whose version you're reading, right? At bottom, who knows why things go down the way they do? Maybe Moses knows. Maybe Ahura Mazda knows. But I don't know. I haven't the faintest idea. The only thing I'm sure of, Nick, is that free will's an illusion. In the big picture, things were always heading in exactly this direction."

"What do you mean?"

"You asked how everything got this fucked up? Well, I'm telling you how," he said. "I was always gonna fuck it up like this is how, and from the very start. There is no evidence that I would ever have done anything else. Philosophically speaking, that which *is* always trumps that which might have been. Have you ever heard of the *ding an sich*?"

"Please." I made a pushing motion with my hands. "Not now, not today."

He shrugged his shoulders. "Just trying to oblige."

We sat a moment.

"Okay," he said quietly, half to himself, "I know that it's weird to hear, but I can bail out my head with thought, and I can live in this little room where maybe it happened but if so it was crucially done by someone else, in some other time, in a parallel universe, maybe, and by a guy who was sorrowing and sad about it but who did it because he had no other choice. I can feel bad for that guy and girl, and I can even want to be their friend too, because I admire their purity of heart. I get this warm sympathetic buzz of thinking how I'll be friends with a dead girl and an outlaw, and how it'll be cool and *Bonnie and Clyde* and like that, and then I snap out of it and realize that I *am* him, and I *did* do that, and I begin to cry like a first-class pussy. I've done a lot of crying recently, if that makes you feel any better."

I was confused. "Why should it make me feel any better?"

For a moment, neither of us said anything. Then he slowly raised his eyes to mine, and from far off, gave me the mildest, gentlest of smiles.

"My life is over," he said.

"No it's not!"

"Yes it is."

"No it's not. Fight back!"

"Like how?"

"Call the DA for starters, Rob. You plead temporary insanity or something, and throw yourself on the mercy of the court. They cut your sentence way down and we go from there. It's a start."

He was looking at me doubtfully. "It's an end, Nick. So they cut my sentence from forty to thirty-five. So what? Do you know what it's like in a state prison? Do you know what it's actually like in those kinds of places? People come out of there with the shapes of their heads changed, singing songs in a language that no one else can understand."

"It's not summer camp, I know that, Rob. But you being you, you could make good on it somehow, write the tell-all book, get the media involved, do the charismatic jailhouse thing, turn it around in some way. I'm sure you could."

Staring at the ground, he shook his head from side to side.

"It ain't happening," he said. Then he looked up at me, squinting. "You know the part in Kafka's letters where he's writing to his fiancée's father, and explaining all the reasons they shouldn't get married? He says that he's irritable and self-involved and gives this whole laundry list of what a shit heel he is? Then he pauses, indents for a new paragraph, and he says, "'At bottom, none of this bothers me in the least, as it's merely the earthly reflection of a higher necessity.'"

"Jesus."

"Well, what we've got here," Rob said, "is one helluva higher necessity."

There was a silence. High in the sky, passing exactly overhead, a plane snored loudly a moment.

"What does that mean?" I asked. "That you had to kill her?"

"Did I ever say I killed her?"

Saying nothing, I shut my eyes, placed my thumb and forefinger on the bridge of my nose, and began squeezing as hard as I could.

"I still can't believe this is happening," I said. "Forgive me for the love of God, but I can't believe it's happening."

"You know what? I can't believe it either," he said. "I haven't believed it from the moment it went down. But the world goes on, and the executioner's horse does, in fact, scratch its innocent behind on a tree."

"What?"

"Just some poem I always loved, about how the world is always going on in its big worldly way, despite your local little hand-wringing bullshit."

"Look"—I leaned forward—"let's get real here. There's tons of people all over this state and probably country who love you, Rob, and would do anything for you, including coming forward to testify. You can use some kind of grief defense. Everybody knows what happened with that guy, Framkin, and I'm sure there are lots of sympathetic jurors out there waiting to do the right thing. You can tell them, who knows, that Shirley beat you with a violin when you were twelve. You can tell them a million things. It's definitely worth a shot."

"Beaten with a violin," he said musingly. "I like that. I love the thought of being descended from a musical sadist."

Looking at him, his face curled into a sardonic grin, I noticed that he looked more alive now, after a week on the lam, frayed by insomnia and exposure, than he'd looked when I'd seen him at New Russian Hall. It was the excitement of it; it was the drama of it; and it was the fact that he was in the middle of it, and administering the terms of it, that gave him strength, I thought.

"Lecture tours, movie tie-ins," he was saying, "hell, if gangbangers can become household names, so can I." He laughed. "God, am I going to miss you, Nick. I don't think I realized how much till just this very second. But it's too late to audition for the rehab to riches story, and nothing I do from here on in is ever gonna land me on a Cheerios box. Being wholesome is gonna have to wait till the next go-round, I'm afraid—"

"Rob, just think seriously a moment—"

"—along with the whole family thing, the inground pool and the little kids who look like fractions of you, running around saying, 'Daddy this' and 'Daddy that.'"

"If we could just think concretely a second," I said loudly.

Rob seemed suddenly startled. "But why?" he asked. "Why should we think concretely? And what's there to think about? I'm not going to make it, Nick, okay? Get it through your well-meaning skull. I'm going down. I'm going down because the shit rises to the top and the cream curdles and rots and the best people you never hear of at all because they stay home, out of the line of fire, and plant their gardens and live their lives. What's right in my case is simply to go. I've thought about this a lot and it's the only thing that makes sense. It's also the best thing I can do to protect whatever crummy literary posterity I have left."

"What do you mean, go?" I asked. "Go where? It's become much harder to do the international-fugitive bit than it used to be, you know. What, like hiding out in the Virgin Islands?"

"That wasn't the going I was thinking of, Nick."

"No? Well, what then?"

"I'm afraid," he said, "there's only one way to square the equation here, and make what I did with Kate mean anything. That way is to remove both parties to the event."

I was still looking puzzled, I guess, because he added simply, "I'd like to die on my own terms, get it?"

From far off, a speck of thought gathered shape and mass until it exploded in my mind as a word: "Suicide?"

He nodded slowly.

"Oh, come off it!"

"Why not?"

"Because you can't! Because it's insane and crazy and wrong in a thousand ways!" I shouted. "Because you're alive, not dead, and you've gotta stay that way! Oh don't even start with that." I was waving my arms. "Don't even think that!"

"You love me," he said, "don't you."

"What?" I put my hands down.

"Well, don't you?"

"Love you? If you need to hear it, yes, of course I do."

"Well, I love you too."

"Good. So?"

"So it's in that spirit, and with that in mind, that I'm telling you all this."

"Well, great," I said. "Well, that's lovely. You like me so much you want me to know that you're planning on killing yourself? That's beautiful, Rob."

"I know it's difficult to swallow," he said, "but there are reasons, and they're important reasons, and in the bigger picture, that's why we've come together today."

He began fishing around in his backpack.

"What are you doing?" I asked.

"I'm procuring exhibit A," he said, withdrawing from the bag a small shiny pistol. He put it on the ground between us. "Otherwise known as My Way Out."

"I'm gonna go now," I said.

"No, stay. Do you remember"——he reached back into the backpack and withdrew a handful of bullets, which he began loading into the pistol with little terminal clicking sounds——"that wicked good lunch your mom used to make for us when we were kids?"

I could feel the function of memory operating as a kind of pulling feeling about the mouth and temples, but I fought it. I said, "What are you doing, Rob?"

"She had this can of chicken gravy, and boiled this white rice to go with it, and poured the one on the other, and you and I, we used to go to your house and eat this stuff, which would barely fit the description of glue, and your mother used to call it chicken à la Framingham, and we loved it. I mean, I used to go home and tell my mother how great it was. Don't you remember that?"

"Yes, I remember it, so what?"

"What about our heists, man, do you remember them?"

At twelve, dressed in studiously casual clothes and carrying under our arms a box carefully crafted so as to appear recently received from the post office, we had slipped into the town's largest record store. The box had a cunningly concealed razor slit in its side, and while one of us distracted the cashier, the other whisked as many albums as possible through that slit and into the box.

"Yes," I said, impatiently, "I do."

"You," said Rob, "were the best sentry a guy ever had."

"Where are you going with this?" I asked.

"Funny," he went on, as if he hadn't heard me, "the way how when you're a kid, childhood feels like prison, but when you're an adult it magically changes into the freest, purest span of time you ever knew. What a swindle, eh?"

"That's true," I admitted.

"And how when you're little you think everything in the adult world is stable and never moving, like furniture, and your parents' lives change with glacial slowness, like the dinosaurs dying over ten million years. And yet when you're an adult, the older you get the faster it moves. You blink your eyes, and bang it's the next year. You wake up from a nap, and dammit if it isn't the very next year."

"Fine, okay. You've now made two points in a row. Congratulations," I said.

"I can't do it."

"Can't do what?"

"I can't do it, Nick." And with that, with no warning at all, Rob's eyes filled with tears. "I've tried for days and days to do it. I've put the muzzle in my mouth, at my temple, in my stomach, I even stuck the damn thing down my pants, but I can't do it."

"You can't do it," I said, "because you still have a shred of sanity left."

"No, man"—the tears were spilling down his face—"I can't do it because I don't have the guts, okay? That's the sad fucking truth—I'm scared."

"Stop this," I said sharply. "You can't do it because it's a sick act and you're not sick. Disturbed maybe, but not sick. Come here." He leaned forward and I cradled him in my arms, and he relaxed into my shoulder, sniffling a little. I said, "This is easy, Rob. This is a no-brainer. You simply march into the police station and present yourself. I'll walk you the whole way."

"No"—he stiffened instantly—"I have to go, Nick." He drew away and looked at me. "I know that this is what I have to do. I *know* it. And I can't pull it off myself. I just can't."

I grew suddenly cold, as a larger suspicion dawned on me. "Wait a minute," I said, "what are you asking me?"

"You're here," Rob said, wiping his running nose on the back of a hand, "in the role of a best friend who's appeared miraculously, because I stayed here specifically in the hope that you would."

"I think I'm going to be sick," I said.

"That's okay," he said.

I held a hand to my mouth, but the nausea passed. "The thing about you," I said, "is that for one brief second I almost believed you. I was almost convinced that you really *should* have your brains blown out. You could talk the rain from a cloud, Rob. I'll mortgage my frigging house to pay your hospital bills if it comes to that, but I'm not helping you with this craziness."

To my surprise, his response was to grab me firmly by the chin with both his hands, lean close and look deep into my eyes.

"Please," he said.

"What?"

"Look at me."

"I am."

"No, *look* at me."

Obligingly, I looked. Those large, midsummer sea-blue eyes I'd first glimpsed over thirty years earlier, responding to a knock on our front door, now widened before me. I'd never before stared into another man's eyes from close up. I'd never felt the strange altering heat of feeling that accompanies such a thing as time passes. We kept holding each other's gaze as he stared calmly back at me, and slowly, a strange process began. His face started to grow abstract, the hard planes of it began to melt and run, and the accustomed perceptual pegs of face, eyes and nose broke into a completely unrecognizable jumble of indistinct pieces that began serially reassembling in waves of new sense. Beneath the haggard worn adult flesh, I believed I could see, suddenly, the face of the cherubic little boy starting up, eager to show off his reading and speak in laughably adult sentences. I could see the shining adolescent, beating all over with hungry pulses, and the long-haired rebel, slouching languid inside some posture of inner rage. There was also a terrifying moment when the same elements assembled abruptly into something dark and monstrous, a grotesquely ill-fitting and ghoulish mask. But this quickly passed, and the planes returned to normal. And yet something had taken place in the interim. Restored to itself,

Rob's face remained filled with a strange, luminous quality, a sparkling intent that seemed to have traveled from all those previous perceptions back to the present tense.

"Let's do it," he said softly.

I felt suddenly very drained, and very tired.

"No, Rob," I said in a flat voice, "I'm sorry, but no."

He sat back away from me. He sighed. He tensed, as if about to say something, then seemed to catch himself and relax again.

"No?" he asked. "You sure?"

"Never."

He shut his eyes for a moment.

"Okay, weakling," I thought I heard him whisper.

"What?" I asked.

"I said you were a weakling." He opened his eyes.

I laughed. "What, because I don't want to go along with your fantasy plan for murder? For that I'm a weakling?"

"No, you're a weakling because you never once in your life had the balls to follow through on the truth of your own perceptions."

I felt the sting of accuracy in what he was saying, and lowered my head.

"You were always jealous of me," he said.

"Maybe." I flung my head back up. "But so what?"

"And you *should* have been jealous of me."

Despite everything, I was suddenly furious. "Ah, now I think I get it. You're going to try to provoke me into killing you, is that it? What is this, a movie of the week? Come on, Rob."

"Poor Nick," he said.

"I'm going to go now," I said.

"No, wait!" To my horror, he then fell to his knees in front of me, placed his hands together, pressed his face into the dirt and raised it, caked with filth, while crying, "Forgive me, Nick! That was a stupid thing to try! I'm coming to you now in simple friendship and love to ask you to perform this little mercy. Mercy! You never understood," he said, "how strong you were—and I need that strength now! You were always better than you knew—and that's the part of you I'm talking to!" Moistly, his eyes rolled up to meet mine, the lashes grimed.

"Please, brother," he said.

"Rob."

"Please!"

"I can't."

"You can!"

"I won't!"

He started crying again, deep, racking, sepulchral sobs, and I looked away and up at the sky, which, as ever, stretched above us with the shell lusters of its distances promising celestial perfections at which our life on earth could only hint. What does loyalty signify? I wondered. What would it mean to follow an idea or a person through the thickets of one's distaste, overriding one's own suspicions and trampling one's core beliefs in the service of some huge, dimly comprehended abstraction like Faith? How might it come to pass, and for what reasons, that a person perfectly in control of his own faculties could be talked, cajoled, beseeched into doing something he fundamentally didn't want to do? We were in the epicenter of our childhood, that place where we'd first flirted with each other in the manner of young boys, trying out our moves, tumbling through our shyness and pride. How was it that Rob, here, for the very last time in his life, was about to get his way?

Tears, and snot running from his nose; his hands hanging at his sides in a way that allowed the sick, sad animal to be seen, with the thin veil of the human soul clinging. And in all of that the constant reminder of our twin paths, lived sometimes at variance, sometimes in common, but leading all the way back to the beginning of shared time.

I picked up the gun.

# chapter 29

"HE WON," SHE SAID SADLY.

"Who did?"

"Rob Castor."

There was a pause. "How do you mean?"

"I mean," said Lucy, "that your relationship with him and his family destroyed this marriage."

I got slowly to my feet from the couch. It seemed the wrong moment to be sitting down. Two large valises stuffed with my clothes and papers lay on the floor alongside me. My car, already started outside, was warming up against the winter chill. A week earlier, with dinner over and the children abed, Lucy had convened a meeting at the kitchen table, and calmly requested a divorce. I had been amazed by the fluency and self-possession with which she stated her case. Since returning home from her sacred intimacy retreat, she'd said, everything was far clearer, as, she'd added crisply, was the path she had to now take. She was big on

"paths" suddenly, and on "the place of achieved honesty."
She had that earnestness in her face that I hadn't seen since
she'd begun boning up on motherhood years earlier, turning our then one-room apartment into a heaped lending
library of books on the subject. We argued slowly and carefully over several days, as she explained that it didn't make
sense to do what we were trying to do, because, at bottom,
both of us were waiting for something to happen that
probably wouldn't happen and maybe shouldn't, if it came
to that. Had there ever been a merge? she'd asked rhetori-
cally. Had there really truly ever been a merge between us?

"The thing about Rob," she went on now as I stood
motionless in the living room, staring at my bulging,
forlorn-looking luggage, "was that you never understood
how he always envied you having me, having the kids,
having all those things you looked down at through his
eyes as dumb and boring and middle class. You didn't realize it, Nick, but at bottom, he envied you bad."

"Rob wasn't the envying type."

"You don't think so? I do. I think he was eaten up with
the stuff. And you always underestimated yourself around
him. You made yourself out to be this boring drudge next
to a guy you thought was a glorious rainbow of a personality, but you were wrong. I've always wanted to tell you
this, and now I can. Rob was just a common hustler with
a gift for language. He also—hello?—happened to be a
murderer. If he ended up dead and buried, that's nobody's
fault but his own. But you seem to have taken the whole
thing personally, like you have to be his official mourner
or something and walk around with a long face for the rest
of your life."

Three days into our "discussion," on bended knee, I'd given a short, passionate speech in which I'd begged her to reconsider. I'd spoken of the children, invoked our long-standing kindness to each other, and excused my recent behavior as a temporary midlife crisis, nothing more. As I spoke I carefully watched her face, trying to gauge the effect of my words on her feelings. A kind of whiteness had clouded her features when I began talking, and it dispersed only when I finished. It was sometime not long after that, looking calmly into my eyes, that she said the word "no." She said many other things, but I don't remember any of them. A kind of arterial roaring had begun in my ears, and as I walked out of the room, I recall repeating to myself hypnotically that everything would be fine, that this was all exactly what I'd wanted, and that in a certain crucial sense it was not she but I who'd initiated the divorce in the first place.

In the days afterward, by common consent, we went out of our way to minimize all public displays of sadness or remorse for the sake of the boys. The children, in fact, seemed by virtue of their own existence to be instructing me in some heavy primary lesson of life. The sheer animal ease with which they ran around in their boots tracking muddy ice through the house, the vital fizz they gave off as they hurled snowballs at each other or slid screaming up and down the local hill on their sleds seemed somehow to point up the sour, imprisoning egoism of divorce. Were we so contracted, Lucy and I, that the natural pleasures of childhood struck us as miraculous?

"I've made you something," she said now, getting up from the couch herself.

"What's that?"

"Some food, Nick, to tide you over."

She went to the fridge, from which she withdrew a big Styrofoam cooler. "A leg of lamb, some pork chops, a few side dishes."

She placed it on the ground between us. There was then a silence during which the desire to cry came over me with such swiftness that I avoided it only by pressing my hands between my knees till the pain made me gasp. When I looked up, tears were streaming down her face.

"You look pale," she said, wiping her eyes.

"I feel pale."

"I know what you mean."

"Dear God," I said simply, and stared at the ground.

Several times, in the previous few days, I'd fallen prey to that particular kind of magical thinking which proposes that with a mere small adjustment or two, it can all be made to go away. Earlier that same evening, struggling to keep my emotions in check, I'd casually bid the boys good night, and had lingered an extra moment, caressing their hair as they lay in bed while feeling that the sheer normalness of my actions would somehow forestall the inevitability of what was coming.

Lucy now reached forward and affectionately adjusted my collar.

"I still can't believe we're doing this," I said in a low voice.

Rather than speak, she simply nodded in a way that seemed both to acknowledge that truth and declare her determination to proceed.

"You know I'll always love the good in you," she said quietly.

I struggled to say something but couldn't find the words.

"And you'll get everything you want in life," she went on. "I'm sure of that. I really and sincerely am. Hold on to that thought. And I'll do likewise. And we'll talk very soon." I leaned forward to kiss her good-bye, and as our lips touched, a cold, sick churning began in my stomach, and more than her kindness or love, I realized at that very moment, it was her body to which I was fatally attached. It was the warm breasts I had held through so many nights, the collarbones that cupped the natural perfume of her skin, the tapering pedestal of her long legs that I was suddenly in an agony of parting from. We hadn't made love for a long time, but no matter. The thought of future trespasses of that body by strangers made me want to howl out loud like a dog. I was glad for the heavy physical weight of the bags in my hands at that moment. They grounded the balloon of my regret, which was trembling with uplift and wanting just then to soar into an attack of full-on congestive sobbing. Keeping a tight hold on myself, I pulled away from Lucy, nodded stiffly, and knowing I'd be screening the film of this moment for the rest of my life, walked out the front door to my car with as much dignity as I could muster. The house with the lighted eyes of its upstairs windows and the brows of its eaves had never looked friendlier, more inviting, and as I drove off it was all I could do not to feel that it was myself I was looking at, the simpler, surer self I'd been when we'd first bought that house, that self whom—as I turned the corner at last and the house slid out of sight—I was certain I would never see again.

I drove along the roads of my hometown slowly, as if grown suddenly unsure of streets traversed ten thousand times. Arrived at the residency hotel, I checked myself in in a kind of trance. I stretched out in the scratchy sheets of my bed, and I closed my eyes. To think was to risk a landslide. Better simply to inhabit the present tense as best I was able. I beckoned sleep to come forward out of the shadows and soothe me, but sleep resisted. I wanted to be blotted out. I wanted to drink oblivion and have it flood me with forgetfulness. I had never completely come to terms with what I had done in the woods six months before, when the shot rang out, and a violent compression of sound, widening upward and climbing fast, was soon dispersed on the heavy, still, hanging summer air. In and around the torn-up places inside myself, I continued to miss Rob. He used to say that nouns were bits of two-sided tape that made symbols stick to life. He once told me all of poetry was contained in the *b* of the word subtle.

Lying in my rented room, I wanted to fast-forward five years and compress all the stumbling, the late-night bone-chewing, the confusion and the pain into the future synthesis of a brisk, purposeful man who cared about new things, and new people. I could feel the soft moment arriving in which sleep would open up like a mouth and swallow me. I would flow through that sleep and wake up a tiny bit better. And each day from here on in would have that much less anguish than the day before, and would be a small stop against the forward current of regret. Because what's past is past, right?

Right?

# acknowledgments

TO BETSY LERNER FOR HER SAGE COUNSEL DURING the gestation of this book, and for her brilliant demonstration of the lost art of editing; to Henry Ferris, the resident genius of William Morrow, for his peerless care, enthusiasm and critical discernment, and to Lisa Gallagher, Tavia Kowalchuk and Seale Ballenger of the Morrow team as well; to Mark Kamine for the myriad ways in which he interpreted the word *support*; to my circle of original writer friends, who over the years have provided a traveling biosphere of sorts—Peter Cole, Martin Earl, Donald Berger, Brian Kitely and Stephen O'Shea; to the fays Susan Bell, Leslie Browne and Nevine Michaan; to Eli and Noah Godec-Rosen for their unchecked irrigation of the heart; and most of all to Judy Godec, my cherished partner in all things, whose light and love sped these pages into being, thank you.